CRAVE

*An Erotic Story
Collection*

By Miranda Silver

COPYRIGHT

To Jan, for the inspiration

CONTENTS

ABOUT CRAVE

Crave is a collection of sensual erotic stories in which lovers explore their deepest fantasies and hidden desires. These short stories are perfect for a bite-sized quickie before bed — or any time you're craving a naughty escape.

"The Wedding and the Wolf" features Patrick Caruthers and Christina Ramirez from my novel *Priceless,* but can be read as a standalone.

This book contains graphic sexual scenes, including light BDSM, Daddy kink, reverse harem, bondage, erotic humiliation, and spanking, as well as steamy vanilla encounters.

100% of the proceeds from *Crave* will be donated to Feeding America.

TROUBLE

Getting dumped is never fun.

But when it's two months before your wedding, it does strange things to a girl.

Which might explain why, late on this hot July night, I'm crouched on the carpet of my old bedroom.

The lights are off, and my nose is pressed to the window. I'm staring at the square of light next door. I'm wearing a tiny tank top and shorts that haven't made an appearance since high school.

And I'm drooling over the sculpted male chest that's framed in that lighted window.

Jake's chest.

This is wrong.

A week ago, I was trying on my wedding dress and making plans for the future with my fiancé, Kevin. Now I'm camped out at my parents' house, licking my wounds.

Squirming on my carpet in the dark.

Ogling Jake Benson.

He's a grown man. When did that happen? He must be past twenty-one now.

I grab the curtain to pull it shut. It's Jake's choice to flaunt his abs through the open window. To stand there unconcerned, the lamplight glowing on his lean, beautiful body. But he doesn't know I'm spying on him.

I used to babysit Jake, for God's sake. Back when being five years older than him meant that I was in charge.

But when I go to tug the curtain closed, an intense twinge between my legs stops me from shutting out the view.

As a kid, Jake was hell on wheels. His parents praised me profusely for being the only sitter who could stand him and his brothers. It helped that they also paid profusely.

Jake was smart, but a rabble-rouser. There was the chemistry experiment that almost blew up the kitchen, the illegal fireworks that he charged the neighborhood kids a fortune to watch him set off. *An experiential learner,* his mom would say, exhausted.

When I went away to college, I wondered about him. The hell-raiser teetering between success and destruction. I had a soft spot for Jake, and I kept my fingers crossed for success.

Now I'm twenty-six, back home, and spying. My love life is in shambles. And Jake is standing directly in front of his window, stretching his muscled arms over his head.

A bulge tents the front of his jeans. He unbuckles his belt, slowly, and I bite my lip. My window's closed, but I can imagine the clink.

When he unzips his fly, I squeeze my legs together. The intricate tattoo on his shoulder catches the light.

I would never be kneeling here, my breath quickening with excitement, every inch the voyeur, if it weren't for this morning.

At six am, the crunch of wheels on gravel woke me. I crept to the window and saw Jake taking his family's trash and recycling bins to the curb.

It was cool out, the summer heat not yet in bloom. But Jake

was shirtless, and his pajama bottoms rode well below his hard waist, showing off the trail of hair pointing toward his crotch. I hadn't realized he was home from college.

I haven't been home much myself the past few years. Busy with grad school and Kevin, who just tossed me aside like a crumpled tissue. *Better to end this now than after the wedding, Ella.*

So I missed seeing Jake transition from boy to man.

And in the quiet morning light, he was magnificent. Lean and graceful, his short brown hair glinting in the first rays of summer sun. His jaw was sharp, his cheekbones defined. A tattoo swirled over his shoulder.

He was full of energy and life, and God, I wanted those right now.

Without thinking, I ran outside barefoot, grabbed our bins from the garage, and dragged them next to Jake's at the curb.

"Hi, Jake," I said breathlessly, like a seventh grader with a crush. "It's been awhile."

His face broke into a grown-up version of his trademark mischievous grin. "Hey, Ella. Too long."

He took me in as I stood in front of him. Braless, my dark hair falling out of its bun, in my tight white tank top and little polka-dotted shorts. His eyes drank in my face and lingered on my breasts.

When I glanced down, my nipples, tight and puckered, poked insistently through the sheer white fabric.

"I guess it's pajama day," I joked, but my laugh caught in my throat.

"Then every day should be pajama day."

"It pretty much has been. I've barely changed out of mine since I got home." I looked away.

"Yeah, I heard your wedding's off. I'm sorry." He put his

11

hand on my shoulder. When did he get taller than me? Like, six inches taller? "He didn't deserve you."

"That's really sweet, but you know absolutely nothing about my ex-fiancé."

"So tell me something to make it true. I hate being a liar." He flashed that teasing grin. Totally ladykiller smile, and he had to know it.

"Fine. Let's see... Right before we broke up, he said he could see me being the mother of his kids, but he couldn't see having sex with me for the rest of his life."

Jake let out a long, low whistle.

Jesus, why did I share that? Flushing hot, I rummaged through the recycling bin. "I'm sorry, that was inappropriate."

"*Wildly* inappropriate. Moms are sexy."

"Jake..."

"You'd be a very sexy mom."

"Okay, okay." I held up my hands, laughing.

"You're sexy without being a mom, too. He's an idiot. And guess what? He didn't deserve you."

"All right. And you're not a liar."

Jake cocked his head, studying me. "I turned twenty-one on Saturday."

"Right. July, I remember. Happy birthday."

"It was. But the party's not over yet. Wanna help celebrate?"

Heat spread from my cheeks to my chest. "How?"

"We go out, I buy you a drink, you tell me more wildly inappropriate things."

Shit. This was dangerous. "Why would you buy *me* a drink for *your* birthday?" I teased.

"You can buy me a drink too if you want. And I can... distract you." His eyes flicked to my hips. My shorts were pushed up, caught between the soft apex of my thighs, outlining the triangle of my pussy. "You seem like you could use some distraction."

Sweet dampness trickled into my panties. Under Jake's gaze, I felt *wanted*. In a way I never had with Kevin.

"I think I better stick to making a blanket fort on the couch and watching Netflix," I murmured.

"Okay." He shrugged. Something flashed in his blue eyes. Disappointment? No, not that. "If you change your mind, let me know."

As I turned and walked to my front door, I felt his gaze on my ass. I knew that glint in his eyes. I'd seen it enough times.

Trouble.

Now, crouching in my darkened bedroom, I stare at the window opposite mine. I spent hours camped in front of the TV tonight, but this show is much, much better.

Jake unzips his fly and eases his jeans down. An obvious bulge tents his boxers.

Then the boxers are off, too.

He's naked, stunning, and aroused. And looking straight at my dark window, his face suffused with lust.

Does he know I'm here?

Is he tempting me?

His cock is gorgeous. Thick, curved, pointing toward me. He grips the shaft, stroking it.

As I cup my own breasts in the dark, rubbing the soft curves through my shirt, I imagine kneeling for him. Taking his cock in my mouth. Swirling my tongue worshipfully over the head as he tells me exactly what he likes.

It arouses me to think of submitting to him, after spending all those years telling him what to do.

"Jake," I moan. I pinch my nipples to tight buds while he leisurely jerks his dick. When his eyes narrow with arousal, my mouth waters.

It's so intimate, sharing this moment with him.

And so wrong, because he doesn't know we're sharing it.

Does he?

Buzzing with excitement, I slide a hand into my shorts. Slickness greet my fingers. I find my sensitive clit and circle the nub faster and faster. I'm so aroused, sensations buzzing through my slippery pussy.

I want to see Jake's orgasm. I want to watch that thick, beautiful cock erupt.

His hand blurs on his shaft. Excitement gathers, tightening as I imagine him seeing me. Penetrating me. Fucking me.

Jesus, Ella, you're beautiful. I'm gonna fuck you so hard...so deep...

This is it. We're going to come together, his cock spurting while I cream my shorts over the hell-raising boy who's all grown up.

Suddenly, he stops. He lets go of his dick, walks to the light switch, and plunges the room into darkness.

A piece of cardboard appears inside his window. Streetlights illuminate the thick black writing:

If you want more, come over and show me yours.

After a minute, it's flipped to the other side: *I'll give you what he never did.*

My heart beats fast.

That sign was pre-made. He's planned all of this. He knows I'm watching, maybe even saw me. The fucking audacity, the nerve...

I jump up to pace my room, but I'm too shocked and excited

to think straight. All I see is his insolent grip on his cock. All I feel is the insistent throb of my pussy.

I slip out of my parents' dark house, careful to avoid the creaky boards in the hallway, and race across the grass. Dew coats the bare soles of my feet.

I'm just going to talk to him. To tell him this is "wildly inappropriate" and needs to stop.

When I round the corner, Jake's waiting outside the gate to his backyard. His eyes spark, as if he weren't sure whether his little game would bring results.

Pulling me into his backyard, onto his family's patio, he catches my arms in his hands, holding me at a distance.

He's wearing boxers, nothing else. The faint moonlight and shadows of the summer night play hide and seek with his lean torso and tattoo. His boxers mask his arousal, but it beats at me from every inch of his skin.

I know exactly how hard his cock is, pushing out the plaid cotton. How sweetly muscled his ass is.

"I guess it's still pajama day." My voice comes out husky. "I never changed."

His gaze travels down my body.

My tank top is pulled down low because I reached inside to touch my breasts. It shows off the soft flesh of my cleavage. My nipples push out the thin fabric, begging to be sucked.

And the crotch of my tight shorts is pushed completely to one side, revealing the mound of my pussy barely covered by silky purple panties. A dark spot shows where my excitement has soaked through.

"Jake," I begin.

"I see you've already gotten a start on showing me yours." He flashes that ladykiller smile. "Nice, Ella. Very nice."

"I'm just here to talk to you." I try to summon a shred of authority, but I don't convince even myself.

"Are you? Or are you here to take your shirt off?"

Silence mounts between us. A vein pulses in his forehead. His blue eyes flicker.

"If you're just here to talk, tell me now. Tell me to let go of you and I will."

"Your family—" I begin.

"Fast asleep."

"You saw me?"

His mouth twitches. "I guessed. I saw you come in your room, turn the light off, and leave the shutters open." When I don't move, when I don't tell him to let go, his smile widens. "I wonder what you were doing in there?"

He knows.

Have I lost my mind? I'm creaming myself in Jake's arms — his big, strong arms — as more juices trickle into my panties.

My skin tightens into goosebumps. Fuck it, fuck it all. I don't care about anything right now except the excitement coursing through my body and Jake's grip on my skin.

I grasp the hem of my tank top and slowly, slowly pull it up, until my breasts spring free.

"Damn," he whispers.

Jake's eyes are glued to the soft, round curves and hard rosy nipples. He releases my arms so I can lift the shirt over my head.

"You're incredibly sexy," he murmurs. "I always knew you were."

"Thank you."

My throat closes. Kevin didn't think I was sexy. He saw me getting softer in the time we were together, saw me as a piece of furniture he could sit on and use. But Jake is hungry, riveted.

16

I hook my thumbs into my shorts and begin to slide them over my hips.

"Not like that," Jake says softly. "Pull your panties out of the way between your legs. Show me how wet you are."

His orders turn me on beyond belief.

Planting my bare feet further apart, I pull the soaked crotch of my panties to one side. The movement exposes my aroused pussy, showing a glimpse of the tender pink folds, shiny with juices. My swollen clit peeks out.

Jake growls, squeezing the erection that tents his boxers. Lust hangs thick in the air. I moan, because it's so erotic.

"Fucking gorgeous," he mutters. "Stay like that." He comes close, one foot between mine, his dick inches from my exposed pussy. "When was the last time you had sex, Ella?"

There's something so personal about the question, and so intimate that he's asking. Stripping away a layer, making the encounter more vulnerable.

"Two months ago. Give or take," I murmur.

"Was it good?" He holds my gaze. "Was it ever good?"

I shake my head. Even in the best times with Kevin, he never looked at me like I was the only drink that could quench his thirst. I never pounced on him in wild abandon.

Jake's voice lowers to a secret. "And so you came home."

My breasts rise and fall. The air between us is charged. "I did."

"You're here at this house where I used to run you ragged. I always knew you liked me, no matter what I did. You never said I was a bad kid. You were sweet to me. Well, I liked you too. Now you've watched me jerk off. You're practically naked. Showing me your beautiful tits and your horny, needy little cunt." I groan as his dirty words wash over me. "Tell the truth,

Ella. What do you want?"

"I want you to touch me."

His face lights up in that smile, and there's that glint in his eye that can only mean trouble.

"I was hoping you'd say that."

His hands cup my face in a moment of unexpected sweetness, then glide down my neck and over my collarbone to my breasts. I suck in my breath as he takes his time fondling and caressing the round curves.

"I've been wanting to do this for a long time." He rolls my nipples between his fingers, tweaking them to points.

"God, Jake, oh God…" My breaths come shallowly.

"Jesus, Ella, you are so *horny.*" The crude words make my pussy spasm. "You're about to turn into a puddle of gush on my patio, and I haven't even touched you below the waist yet." I reach out for him, and he stops me. "No, don't let go of your shorts. Keep showing me your pussy. Do you like when I tell you what to do?"

"Absolutely."

"Good." He grins. Definitely trouble. "Because I've *always* wanted to boss you around."

He brushes his fingertips over my belly, making me shiver. Then he takes hold of the elastic waistband of my shorts.

"Allow me. I've been thinking about doing this since this morning."

I let him peel off my shorts. I'm so turned on that my juices cling to my panties as he skims them down my thighs. Naked, I snag my fingers in his boxers. They're on the floor in seconds. And Jake is bare in front of me, showing every inch of skin.

"You're beautiful," I breathe. "I love looking at you."

His cock jerks as I stare, thick and veined.

"Just looking?" His voice is strained, his muscles clenched. He's holding back now. Waiting for my next move.

"And touching."

I run my palms over his shoulders, his chest. His skin is hot, smooth, and I wander over the dusting of hair on his chest and his tiny hard nipples. My fingers dip down his abs, seeking what I want most.

Finally, I stroke his hard, hard cock, velvety and big in my hands.

He groans, thrusting forward in response. Eager. Young.

I lean into him and we kiss. It's sudden and surprising and sweet. He lifts my chin with his fingers as our tongues brush. When he cups my mound, I moan into his mouth. Fingers slide into my folds, finding my clit and flirting with my opening.

"What do you want, Jake?" I murmur when our mouths finally separate.

"To fuck you." His breath brushes my ear. "Duh."

I snort with laughter. He kisses my cheeks, my nose, my eyelids.

"I want to fuck you, Ella. I want to bury my cock in you and fuck you into next week." His voice is charged.

God, his free hand is cupping my breast, pinching my nipple harder and harder. Any good sense I had was left at the curb with the trash bins this morning. I can't stop caressing his hot cock and heavy balls.

"I know I gave you hell when I was a kid." He drags his tongue over my neck. "Let me make it up to you."

I'm panting, answering with my own tongue, sucking the salty skin on his neck until he curses and grips my pussy. I take his earlobe between my teeth.

"Will you make me come?" I whisper.

"Jesus, yes. You have to ask?" He swears under his breath. "Damn right I will."

"I want to fuck you too, Jake."

He kisses me again. And again it's so sweet. We're panting for each other, we both want it, but he's not jumping on me — yet. Finally, he breaks free, his blue eyes glazed like he's drunk.

"Lie down." He points to the glass-topped patio table.

"Which way?" I ask saucily.

"On your back." He's flushed, grinning like he just won the lottery. "Spread your legs for me."

He helps me up and opens my legs even wider once I'm sprawled on the hard surface.

It's the same table that's always been here. Memories from ten years ago push up against now. I focus on the man in front of me, whose eyes gleam with mischief that he finally gets to call the shots.

Bending down, he sucks on one puckered nipple, then the other, until they're tight and aching. I dig my fingers into his lithe back.

"Oh God…"

He kisses my stomach, stroking my thighs over and over.

"Please," I gasp.

He slowly spreads my pussy open, gliding his thumbs along my outer lips, until I'm ready to scream.

"Now, Jake."

One finger teases the sensitive tip of my clit.

"Since when do you have this much patience?"

He lifts his head and grins. "I don't. But it's worth it to hear you beg."

He buries his face in my pussy.

I shriek and bite my fist as he sucks on my clit. A hot tongue pushes against my tight entrance, lapping up my juices. When he fills me with his fingers, I slide my hands into his hair. I try not to make too much noise.

I'm so aroused, and he's so good, that my excitement builds fast. I rush closer and closer to the peak. His fingers press hard against my G-spot, twisting and fucking. His soft tongue licks my clit relentlessly, over and over, until I come with a gasp, shoving my pussy into his face.

He doesn't let go. Doesn't stop licking me through my spasms of pleasure. Not until I sigh his name and drop back against the table.

As I fall, he straightens. He gazes down at me, looking very pleased with himself. His lips are glazed with my juices.

"I can't decide," he says softly, resting his palms on my legs to keep them open, "whether to fuck you face-to-face, or take you on your hands and knees. I've thought about it both ways."

"Why choose?"

"I like the way you think, Ella. Scoot to the edge of the table."

My skin is damp with sweat. I wriggle across the table until my ass is on the edge. God, we're outside, we're in his backyard, someone could walk out here any second…

Then he pulls my ass up against his crotch, squeezing the softness in his hands, and I forget about thinking. The tip of his cock presses against my pussy, broad and determined, and I let out a gasp when he penetrates my wetness.

"Fuck," he groans. "Ella…"

He sinks into me, working his way little by little. I reach up to clutch his sculpted shoulders. I'm tight, but so slick that soon he's fully buried in my cunt. He leans his weight against me, his muscles flexed, his hands braced on the table.

21

As exciting as it is to take him inside me, it's the way he says my name, the look in his blue eyes as they lock on mine, that drive me crazy.

"Jake." His name spills out. I press my forehead to his arm, and he growls.

"Look at me while I fuck you."

I obey. I'm in his hands and I love it. I love the thrill of naughtiness from taking Jake inside me. I love that the tables are turned after all these years. I love letting him call the shots.

He thrusts hard, drinking in my gasps and cries like he's been starving for them. The only sounds he's been wanting to hear. It's sharp and sweet and good and I squeeze down on his thick cock, wanting his release…

He pulls out, panting.

"Get up."

I push myself unsteadily to a sitting position, grab the hand he offers, and climb off the table. Naked, pulsing, giddily aroused.

"Turn around. Hands on the table."

His orders are clipped, like he can barely find the words right now. I do as he says.

Hot hands pull my thighs apart, and my palms flatten on the glass table. I moan as he strokes my pussy, peeling open the swollen folds.

Then the blunt head of his cock finds my opening and sinks into my cunt.

The patio blurs. I grip the table as it wobbles and shakes. He's absolutely pounding me, harder and faster than anyone ever has before. It's so intense that I can't fuck him back. I can only be fucked. Smashed, about to explode.

When he comes, he roars. I shudder with pleasure, feeling

the slap of his balls against my pussy.

Finally, his thrusts slow. When he pulls out, my pussy grips him tight, wanting to keep him there. I let out a sigh once he's gone. His cum oozes down my thigh, and I shiver when he kisses my shoulder.

"Jesus Christ," he whispers. "You okay?"

I nod, because talking feels like too much right now. I lean over the table, trying to catch my breath. My heart is pounding a thousand miles an hour.

"So good, Jake," I manage.

He runs a finger down my spine. It traces the curve of my ass as if he has every right to. As if he's free to touch me wherever, however he pleases.

"So…" he begins. and the word hangs there. I realize that after all his recklessness and audacity tonight, after he's just fucked the shit out of me, he's nervous. Because he can't read me from the back. "Are you gonna spend all day in your pajamas again tomorrow?"

I turn to face him and reach up to stroke his shoulders. "I might, if it ends like this."

That troublemaking grin lights up his face.

"Or maybe I'll put on actual clothes and buy you a birthday drink," I continue.

"Maybe you will. Or maybe you'll let me treat you, now that I'm legal." He leans close. "And I can…distract you some more."

"I hope you will," I giggle, and hug him around the neck. His lean, hard body feels so good against my soft curves. He leans against the table, watching with the telltale glint in his eye as I put on my tank top and shorts.

I kiss him on the lips. "Sleep tight," I murmur, and begin to walk away.

"Ella?"

I stop and turn. He's still leaning against the table, naked. Something tells me Jake has an exhibitionist streak.

"Yeah?"

"Do you still have that blue dress?"

I raise my eyebrows.

"You know the one. Little light blue dress with buttons down the front that always looked like they were going to pop. You wore it all through the end of high school and when you came home in the summers from college."

My cheeks turn warm. I do know the dress in question. I haven't worn it since I started dating Kevin. He thought it was too short, too low-cut…too frivolous. *Act your age, Ella.*

"Of course I still have it."

"Wear it when we go get drinks."

The order warms me like a trickle of alcohol down my throat, fizzing in my belly.

"I will."

When I look back over my shoulder as I leave, he's smiling. And in that smile, there's the promise of a hell of a lot of trouble.

DADDY ISSUES

Daddy! Oh God, fuck me, Daddy!

I yank my pillow over my head, but it does nothing to hide the noises from next door. The walls are thin in this building.

It's after midnight, and an unprecedented series of moans and groans have been spilling from my neighbor James's apartment. Now that we're into the wee hours, the dirty talk is kicking into high gear.

And it's making me wet.

Please, Daddy, shove it in me.

I have a case going to trial in the morning, for God's sake. My briefcase and purse sit on a chair next to the suit hanging on my closet door. I need to clear my head and get some fucking sleep, but all I can hear are another girl's moans.

All I want is to be in her place.

Daddy, ow. OW! Ooooh, that hurts so good.

My thighs part, and I stroke my damp pussy. My fingers slide to my swollen clit. I'm in a state of shock that my nice, polite neighbor, a forty-something guy who's a chef at a fancy restaurant, is into this kinky shit.

James is fit. He wears cute little glasses. His brown hair is touched with gray at the temples, and his hazel eyes crinkle adorably when he smiles.

But I bet he's not smiling right now. His face is contorted with lust as he looks down at me — no, her. Thrusting…pounding…maybe slapping. Would he do that?

A Tinder hookup. That's my best guess. She's half his age and I saw them introduce themselves right outside his door.

Make me your SLUT, Daddy!

Jesus. I can't concentrate. She keeps jolting me out of my own fantasy. Maybe it's because the dirty talk sounds so chipper. So oddly impersonal.

Checking the time on my phone, I chuck it onto the nightstand. I can't perform on less than six hours of sleep anymore, much less bounce out of bed bright-eyed and bushy-tailed.

I'm thirty-five years old, I don't have time for this shit.

I roll out of bed, my pussy throbbing for release. I'm tired. I'm annoyed. And I'm dangerously excited to think of James all dominant and mean in bed. Precisely because he's always been such a good neighbor.

Whenever he bakes, which is basically every weekend, he leaves a plate of goodies on my doorstep. He invited our entire floor for a dinner party when he moved in, featuring spaghetti carbonara that caused me to die several ecstatic deaths and really good Chianti. He gets the paper delivered and always gives me the Sunday Times when he's finished. He even leaves the crossword for me.

I've had a crush on James for months and done nothing about it. Because we're both consumed by our jobs. Because we're neighbors. Because he's ten years older.

And now he's screwing someone literally young enough to be his daughter.

26

Who's screaming too loudly to let me sleep or fantasize.

Uhhh! Yeah Daddy, spank me! Harder, harder!

Stomping across my apartment, I grab my stereo speakers and drag them right up against the offending wall. I cue up the sassiest, perkiest dance music I can find and crank the volume way, way up.

Then I let out my frustration in a one-girl dance party — flailing, shimmying, singing at the top of my lungs.

It doesn't take long. In under a minute, there's a firm, pissed-off knock at my door.

Rap. Rap.

I switch off the music and catch a glimpse of myself in the full-length mirror as I go to answer that ominous knock. My short dark hair is practically standing on end. I rake my fingers through it.

My heart is pounding, and it accelerates when I open the door to see James. Shirtless, wearing plaid boxers and the body God gave him. No sign of the glasses.

He's in excellent shape. The man has done good things with the material he's been given. His hair is damp with sweat, and irritation rolls off him.

"Can I help you?" I chirp.

His eyes drift to the mess of my curly dark hair, then down to my bare shoulders. I cross my arms, which pushes up my ample cleavage in my short, sheer lilac nightie.

I'm tall and curvy — thick. No one would call me a little girl by any stretch of the imagination. But I suddenly want to be one for James, and it takes my breath away.

"Care to explain the meaning of that loud music after quiet hours?" he asks, low and curt. "You're a lawyer, Kori. You know what the noise ordinances are."

Oooh, do I love that lecturing tone. Even if it's left over from the show in his bedroom.

"I'm sorry." I widen my eyes. "I just couldn't sleep, what with all the noise coming from *your* place. It was so distracting, I had to put on my favorite song to drown it out."

His mouth opens and closes.

"I apologize," he finally says. "I didn't realize the walls were that thin."

"Don't worry," I assure him. "I didn't hear you. Just her."

His eyes darken. He says nothing.

"She's awfully bossy, isn't she?" I ask sweetly. "Considering you're the one in charge."

Now his gaze travels over me. I uncross my arms to let him see how hard my nipples are through my nightie. Two dark buds ready for him to capture and cruelly twist. A trickle of juice slips down my thigh, because it feels so exciting — so dangerous — to be exposed to him. Especially since there's another girl waiting back in his room. My panties are still lying in my bed, and I know he can see the dark vee of my pussy through my nightgown.

"*Are* you in charge, James?" I ask softly. "Because if this is going to be a regular occurrence…"

He drags his eyes back to my face. "It won't be. If you're ever bothered again, please ring my doorbell instead of resorting to measures that disturb the entire building."

I cock one hip, resting my hand on it, and flutter my lashes. "Yes, Daddy."

He does a slow blink. Then his face changes completely. His eyelids lower, and a faint smile tugs the corner of his mouth.

"Don't sass me, Kori," he says softly.

"Or what?"

The question hangs between us. Our eyes lock.

"What'll you do if I misbehave again? Will you *punish* me?"

That smile quirks his lips, sinister this time, and he tucks it away.

"I just might." Over his bare shoulder, he adds, "Don't try me."

As he walks to his door, I stare at the sexy planes of his shoulders and back. His firm ass. When the door closes with a click, I stumble into my own apartment and dive in bed.

Now my pussy is slick. I squirm and moan, getting tangled up in the sheets. Rubbing my clit in frantic circles, I slide my fingers inside my eager cunt. So excited for James, begging for his attention.

All is quiet from next door, and I stifle my own noises in the pillow. Out of courtesy for the neighbors.

"Daddy," I whimper. "Show me how to behave."

Oh, I will, little girl.

I haven't been a little girl in decades. But I want to be, for him.

*

For the next week, I bide my time. There are no further visits from Tinder Girl. No moans or *Oh Daddys* from James's apartment.

I focus on work, but every night, I feel James over me. Behind me. Surrounding me. Taking charge, punishing me, while I moan in embarrassment and delight. I rub myself like mad, coming on my fingers in orgasms that only leaving me wanting more.

Wanting him.

On Sunday, I get my chance. I hear a thump on my doorstep in the afternoon. When I open the door, there's James's Sunday paper, all neatly folded and ready for me to enjoy. I page through it feverishly.

But it's just a newspaper. There's no sign that anything other than good-neighborliness has passed between us.

I open to the crossword, which he always leaves blank. I'm hoping for some message. Maybe "Be a good girl, Kori" scrawled in the first few spaces. "Or else." But there's nothing.

His silence riles me up, even though the ball is clearly in my court.

I scribble my own message in the crossword, heedless of the spacing.

Oh Daddy James, I can't help but be bad. I try so hard, but I keep touching my little pussy and thinking of you. I need your discipline. I need your COCK. Please, Daddy.

Holy shit. I'm not a shy girl, but I've never been this brazen. Before I lose my nerve, I march across the hall to his door and rip the paper apart.

Page after page of the Sunday Times flutters into the air and lands on his welcome mat. I'm so bratty, I take my own breath away. It's an unbelievable mess.

As a crowning touch, I leave the crossword on top like a cherry for him to pick. I consider folding it, for decency's sake, but don't.

Then I ring his bell three times, quick, and dash into my own apartment, giggling like a madwoman.

Rap. Rap.

I open the door, all innocence. James towers in front of me, his arms folded.

"Yeeessss?" I carol.

"Kori." His eyes are hard behind his glasses. It's a James I've never seen before; the lecture last night was just a glimpse. "Did you make that spectacular mess in front of my door?"

"Yes, Daddy," I murmur. Just saying the word makes me shiver. "What are you going to do about it?"

"Be back at my door in five minutes," he barks, with no trace of a smile on his face. "Oh, and take off those ratty sweats and put on a pretty dress for me. Don't even think of being late."

He walks away and closes his door firmly.

I gasp, heat washing my cheeks. I've never been spoken to that way. If it were anyone else, I'd give them a verbal backhand they'd never forget.

But James's words leave me tingling. Hot. Aching for his hands all over my body.

Off come the comfy gray sweatpants and law-school hoodie I lounge around in on the weekends. I rush to my closet and yank out my dresses for consideration. Most of them say *power. Take me seriously. No nonsense here.*

Finally, I pull out a pale yellow sundress from the back — an impulse buy — and slip it over my head. It's patterned with sunflowers. Sweet and girly, it bares my arms, hints at my cleavage, and comes to mid-thigh.

Perfect. I finger-comb my hair and whip out the lipgloss, pouting at the mirror. Then I dash to James's apartment and knock — politely.

He opens the door. Instead of ushering me in, he stands in the doorway and lifts my chin with one finger.

"Are you sure about this, Kori?" he asks very softly. "Do you want to be punished? By me?"

Thank God the hall is empty.

"Yes," I whisper.

"What's your safe word?"

Excellent question. If only I could think straight right now.

"Chianti," I blurt, spying the wine rack behind him.

He nods. His voice hardens. "Clean up the mess you made."

Not what I was expecting. My cheeks burn as I bend over to gather the spilled newspapers and stuff them in the paper bag he's set out.

I know he can see my panties as my short dress rides up. He can see the dampness, my excitement through the silky fabric — all for him. I let him look instead of kneeling down.

James stands with his arms folded, radiating disapproval, as I hustle to clean up. But the tent in his sweatpants — *he* didn't feel obliged to change — makes it clear that he's enjoying the show.

When his welcome mat is spick and span, he takes the bag and opens his door.

"In you go."

I scurry inside and the door closes behind me with ominous finality.

"Stand on the carpet." He points to his immaculate cream-colored carpet. "There."

My face flames. I do as I'm told.

James circles me, inspecting my body from every angle.

"Very good."

With one finger, he tugs down the strap of my light dress to expose my bra. I shiver from the fleeting touch.

"Take your bra off. You don't need that here."

Holy shit. One touch on my shoulder and he's telling me to take my bra off?

Flushing, I unzip my dress partway and slide the straps off my shoulders. I duck my head girlishly, letting my curly hair fall over my face, as I unhook my bra.

"Look at me, Kori," he orders. "Don't take your eyes off me."

A whimper escapes my lips. I'm already unbearably aroused. I raise my head to meet his hazel eyes, which are narrowed in concentration. On me. Only me.

Slowly I peel off my bra and let the lacy cups fall to the floor, baring my breasts.

"Later, you'll pick that up," he says softly. "Right now, don't move."

I hold onto my pretty yellow dress, bunched around my waist, as he stares at my heavy breasts. He traces one finger over my tight, sensitive nipple, teasing the dark bud, and I jump. When his warm hands close over my breasts, a long, wanton moan drops from me.

"Such sweet little tits," he murmurs. "I'm very pleased."

I squirm, crossing my legs, trying to rub my thighs together. "Little" is the last word that's applicable here. And yet it's so fucking perfect at the same time.

I cry out as he cups my breasts fully, massaging them. Too soon, he lets go.

"Put your dress back on and get over my knee."

Jesus. Oh, Jesus. I scramble to obey, zipping up my flimsy dress up to cover my bare tits.

James sits down on his couch in his T-shirt and sweatpants like he has all the time in the world. Meanwhile, I'm shaking with arousal and we've barely started. Trembling, I lie across his lap, my ass curving into the air.

In a sudden, breathtaking motion, my panties are pulled down to my knees.

Slap! Slap!

He spanks one round cheek, then the other. Over and over. Faster and faster. Not hard, but enough to sting.

"This is what Daddy does when you've been a bad girl," he says, in that low, menacing voice. More spanks. As I wriggle, he drops a firm arm across my waist to keep me in place. "This is what you need. Have you ever gotten the discipline you deserve, Kori?"

"Never," I quaver, shuddering with arousal.

"Then we have a lot of making up to do for such a naughty girl."

"No, Daddy, I'm good," I moan, and it turns into a gasp when his big hand slides between my legs.

"What do we have here, baby girl? I'm feeling a very wet, horny little pussy. Don't tell me you're turned on by your punishment. Are you creaming yourself on my lap because I'm *spanking* you?" Knowing fingers stroke my clit. I wriggle against him, angling my ass for more of his touch. I gasp when one finger gently probes my pussy, massaging the opening. "My, what a naughty little cunt you have." Another slap reddens my ass, just as a second finger works into my pussy, penetrating me, opening me. "Aren't you tight. Let me in, baby."

I moan with need. More spanks rain down on the curvy cheeks of my ass. James's hand on my pussy feels so good, and his hand on my ass stings so bad. I'm caught on a tightrope between pain and pleasure.

"Horny little girls deserve to be taught a lesson." His voice is soft and dangerous. "Especially my little girl."

My head bounces up. I peek over my shoulder.

"Oh really? *Your* little girl? I'm yours?"

He breaks character for an instant, his face startled, then flooded with the sweet grin I know and love. It warms me with delicious heat, making me crave whatever he has to give.

Then his eyes narrow, and his words smolder.

"Absolutely. You came over. You put yourself in my hands. You're offering your delectable body to me. Every inch of it, to toy with and punish as I please. I've been wanting you for months, never dreaming you would have such naughty, slutty, *dirty* little needs. You're mine now. And do I ever have my work cut out for me."

I'm panting, swept up in the current of his words. He's offering so much, and I want it all.

One last smack lands on my ass. My panties are tugged over my ankles and tossed on the floor with my bra.

"Get up. Take your dress off."

I rise unsteadily, soaked and excited. Shaking, I unzip my dress and let it fall to the cream-colored carpet. James grips my hand and leads me naked into his bedroom.

The curtains are drawn. The room is dark, with only a few flickering candles for light. He must have taken those five minutes to prepare too. Beside the bed is an oddly shaped padded table, covered in a soft cloth. I can't stop looking at it.

"Lie face-down on the table, baby girl," he says softly.

He helps me up. It's something like a massage table — if a massage table had a dip where your knees go. My legs are below my upper body, but supported. My puffy nipples rub against the soft cloth. My toes curl, and I clutch the front of the table.

"Spread your legs. Show Daddy your pussy."

I obey instantly, wanting him to see how turned on I am.

"Now hold very, very still."

Rope, smooth but strong, quickly binds my wrists and ankles to the table's legs. My elbows are bent, so I can lift my head and upper body, but the restraints don't budge.

I'm a little scared, and it only sharpens my need. My pulse is pounding. Even though I'm tethered, I feel like I'm flying.

"Look at that luscious pussy." A wet slap lands on my sensitive flesh. It strikes my clit, and I gasp. "Just begging to be filled."

"Please, please…" I babble.

Something big and firm presses against my tight opening. His cock? No, it's too hard. Too smooth. I buck as the toy pushes into me, but there's nowhere to go. James twirls it, working it in and out one agonizing inch at a time. My pussy gets more and more slippery to accommodate the girth of the toy.

It's probably no thicker than a cock. But the shape and the angle — and the many months since I've had sex — all combine to make it seem huge.

It's so fucking good. So full.

"Good girl," he croons. "Taking all of that in your naughty little cunt." He strokes my ass, opening the rounded cheeks. "Now it's time for you to really learn your lesson."

I cry out when cool, slippery lube squirts onto my asshole. A rubbery tip probes the dark pucker.

"Sshhh. Trust Daddy."

His order, confident and reassuring, is exactly what I need. I sigh and relax, yielding as James slowly, firmly pushes the plug into my ass. It's slick with lube, and my ass is so sensitive, alive to the size as it flares out, then narrows and settles in place.

"How do you feel, sweetheart?"

"Stuffed," I moan.

He laughs softly. I can't believe how full my pussy and ass are. It's arousing and uncomfortable and just this side of too much. I'm beyond wet, my clit begging for his touch, and as he massages my ass, teasing my pleasure higher, I try to squirm in my bonds.

But he's tied me so securely, I can't. I'm scared and safe and shatteringly aroused all at the same time.

"James…" I gasp.

"Kori," he murmurs. "Sweetheart."

Then he turns on the vibrator in my pussy. And he starts spanking me again.

He builds up, but it's quickly overload. I'm sobbing, sweating, my hair plastered to my forehead as he sets my body aflame. The sensations blur together. He's everywhere, filling me, striking me, possessing me inside and out. He's giving me so much, more than I ever thought I could take, and yet I crave him. My need for him takes me over.

Sensations break the surface: my soaking cunt, clenching the buzzing vibrator, on the exquisite edge of coming. My sensitive asshole, eagerly clutching the plug. My needy tits, nipples tight and aching, pressing against the soft cloth and firm table. My wrists and ankles, straining their bonds. James's palms, schooling me over and over as he smacks my ass.

When he stops, my cheeks quiver and smart with hot, glowing aftershocks.

The only sound is my panting — and his. He steps in front of me, naked to the waist and soaked in sweat. His short hair is plastered down, the touches of gray glinting in the dim light.

Our eyes lock. We say nothing.

He sheds his sweatpants.

His engorged cock, flushed red, springs out and brushes my full lower lip. A hand grabs my hair, the big palm covering the back of my head.

He doesn't have to give an order. I know exactly what he

needs.

His cock is deliciously thick and hot. I suck eagerly, swirling my tongue over his veined shaft, tasting his satiny skin, lapping up the salty precum at his firm, curved tip. He gasps, his control straining at the seams. I want to savor James, but he's fucking my mouth, his rhythm jerky.

"Look at you, Kori." His growl raises a tremor through my tight-strung body. "Filled completely and still so hungry." His voice drops as I suck harder. "I don't know if you can ever be good."

I raise pleading eyes to his.

"But when you look at me like that..." He cups my face, caressing my cheek. His gentleness is such a contrast to the fat cock fucking my mouth, the thick vibrator buried in my pussy, the plug filling my quivering ass. He takes my face in both hands, and I moan, my lips stretched around his cock. "You have me wrapped around your little finger, don't you, baby? My little girl."

So close, so fucking close to coming from his words...

He pulls his cock free of my mouth. Naked and sexy, he walks behind me. I sob as he teases my swollen lips with a feather touch. Turning off the vibrator, he eases it out of my soaked pussy. Tears are running down my cheeks now because it's all so intense. When he fondles my engorged clit, I snarl, trapped beneath him. He twists the plug in my ass, setting off sparks.

"Please." It's a bare whisper, a mere rasp from me.

"It's okay now, baby. Daddy's here."

Then his cock, warm and hard and alive, runs along the length of my pussy. The head nestles against my overstimulated entrance, and he sinks in.

I cry out because he's so much and so good. He fucks me in short thrusts. Warm fingers surround my clit, tweaking the tender bud until I scream. It doesn't take long before need curls deep in my belly, tightening, tightening.

My orgasm rolls over me in a thunderclap. I climax on his thick cock, spasming around the plug in my ass.

He hisses a stream of dirty words, too filthy to distinguish, coating me in desire. He's so big, and he's thrusting deeper and deeper, possessing me completely. Finally, he groans, burying himself inside me as he finds release.

Suddenly, he pulls out, and I hear the unmistakeable sound of his hand furiously jerking his cock, soaked in my cream. Two last jets of hot cum hit my swollen clit and tender opening.

"Mine," he rasps. Fingers massage his spunk into my clit and push it into my cunt. I tighten helplessly on those fingers that keep taking and taking and taking. "Show me what you're made of, baby girl. Give me your pussy one more time."

"James— Oh God—"

"That's it, sweet one. You can do this. Come for Daddy."

I climax in one long wave, cresting and falling. It carries me above the room and slams me into the table. Obliterating me. Dropping me back in my body.

I'm suspended in a haze. I feel James's lips pressing against my ass and along the length of my back as he loosens the restraints on my ankles and wrists.

His words slip through the haze. "Now you really are my little girl."

"Damn right." My voice is cracked.

He helps me into bed, massages my wrists and ankles, and gives me water to sip.

My head drops to his chest. His sheets are soft and clean-smelling, and everything I want now is right here.

"I've been so busy with work," I finally rasp. "I let everything else go. I liked you for so long and did nothing about it. I feel like I just came alive today."

"Me too."

"Oh?" I give him a sassy smile. "What about your Tinder date?"

He groans. "I needed a release. It was never going to be more than a one-night stand."

"Listen, honey." I nuzzle his sweaty neck. "If it weren't for that girl, I'd be sitting alone in my apartment right now, in my apparently *ratty* sweats, doing the crossword. I owe her a debt of gratitude."

"Is that so?" His eyes gleam evilly. "How grateful are you feeling?"

"James!"

"Just teasing. You're all mine."

"That's the way I like it." When I curl up in the crook of his arm, it feels right. Like we've been doing this for a long time.

And like it's only just begun, glorious and new.

"Kori..." he rumbles, his chest beneath my cheek.

"Yes, Daddy?" I ask innocently, relishing his quick inhalation.

"Why didn't you finish the crossword earlier?"

I blink. I have nothing to say.

"I know you pride yourself on that. I'd even call you..." He runs his fingers through my hair. "...competitive."

"I guess I got distracted," I try.

"I know you, sweet girl, and the last thing you are is distractible. Now, I'm going to give it to you later, and I want you to fill every square. Tell me your dirty fantasies, baby.

Daddy wants to know."

As wrung-out as my body is, I shiver with pleasure.

"Then you're going to need a lot of Sunday papers." He kisses the top of my head as I murmur, "I hope you're ready."

ALL THE THINGS YOU ARE

"I've always wanted to blow the entire lacrosse team."

Damian chokes on his beer at my words. It's just the two of us in the hot tub. Tonight's party is winding down, and everyone else is inside.

"*I'm* on the lacrosse team," he says.

His arm rests along the edge of the hot tub. His fingertips are an inch away from my shoulder. We're sitting close, but not too close.

"Oh, are you?" I stretch luxuriously, water soaking my red bikini top. "Yeah, I guess you are."

I met Damian on the first day of college. Freshman year, we lived across the hall from each other. It's been three years, and I've always seen him as a friend — nothing more. He usually has a girlfriend, though not at the moment.

And me? I prefer to be unattached.

But now, I look him over. His firm shoulders, the water dripping down his chest, his cute curly dark hair that could use a cut. His fingers that can't stay still on the rim of the hot tub.

He shifts in the water. I wonder if he's getting hard.

"Can you…elaborate?" His eyes flick to my face, then away.

"Of course. They're all — excuse me, *you're* all lined up in the locker room. You're sitting on a bench in one long row. Naked. Rock hard." I watch his expression. Tough to tell in the dark backyard, but I swear his cheeks are reddening. "It's silent. No one can talk unless I say so. No one can touch me unless I say so. You're all so fucking desperate to come, desperate for my attention, and I'm the only one who can give it to you. It's just, oh my God, this forest of cocks, and I'm sucking on all of you, and it's more cock than I can even imagine…"

I laugh, kicking my legs in the water.

He looks stunned. "You are so drunk, Alana," he murmurs.

You're so turned on, Damian.

"Maybe." I give a little shrug. "But in this fantasy, everyone is stone cold sober."

I lean across him in the hot tub to get my beer, allowing the tip of my breast to brush his shoulder. Then his cheek. He sucks in a breath.

It's cruel, to tease like this. But I can't stop. It's too much fun.

"What's in it for you?" He smiles, but his eyes are glazed. "Don't you want pleasure too?"

I move closer — just a bit. The hot water foams around us.

"There's lots in it for me. I get attention. I get control. I get masturbation material that will last me *years*. I come better when I'm alone, anyway."

I don't tell Damian that alone is the only way I come.

"You're a tease, aren't you?"

"I guess." I tilt my head to sip my beer. "But this is a dream that's never going to happen. I've resigned myself to that. My favorite fantasy will always be a fantasy."

"You sound very sure about that," he murmurs.

The stars look so pretty overhead. I squint up at them.

"Of course I'm sure. It would be crazy to try it in real life.

There's no guarantee that the guys would be respectful, that they wouldn't gossip or secretly tape it. That it would go the way I want it to."

"Why lacrosse?" His fingers brush my shoulder, and I tense. It feels good, but I'm not asking him to hit on me.

"Oh, you know." I toss back my long wet hair.

"No, I don't know." He's looking at me more intently. "Enlighten me."

"Football's a cliche. Basketball players would never sit still. Soccer players...don't get me started on soccer players."

Damian blows out a breath, stretching his arms in front of him. His cheeks are flushed. He's definitely turned on.

"I get it, Alana. It's all the things we aren't."

"No," I giggle. "It's all the things you are." I sink below the surface of the hot tub until my head is submerged in warm water.

*

Two days later, in the middle of a lecture, my phone buzzes with a text from Damian.

Call me.

I immediately feel tingly, surprised by the fizz of excitement. I mean, it's just Damian. After the party, he walked me home and made sure I got inside okay, because he's sweet like that. And I teased him some more on the way home, because I'm a bitch like that.

I didn't expect him to linger on my mind afterward.

I wait till I'm back in my room to call. He answers with a question.

"Do you want your fantasy to come true?"

My stomach flips. "What are you talking about?"

"The fantasy you told me about in the hot tub, with the lacrosse team."

"I know what you mean. I'm asking about the coming true part."

He exhales. "I know some guys."

"What?" I sit down on my bed, fast.

"Not the whole team, I definitely wouldn't recommend that. But part of it. These are decent guys. They'd be down for this, but respectful."

My mouth opens and closes, but no words come.

"You'd be in control. I didn't tell them your name. To them, it's hypothetical. And, uh, not in the locker room. But that's better as fantasy anyways. You wouldn't actually want to do it in the locker room."

There's a long silence.

"Damian, are you for real?" I finally ask.

"Look," he says quickly, "I'm offering. But I know you didn't ask for this, and I totally get it if you're not interested. Just say so, and we'll never talk about it again."

Holy shit.

He's offering to make my craziest fantasy a reality.

I don't doubt the guys would be respectful; Damian would make sure of that.

I'm in shock, and I can't answer right away. Because my vision swims with a group of nameless hot men, naked and straining and desperately turned on. Needing the relief that I can give them.

And one man who's definitely not anonymous.

I catch my reflection in the mirror. My long brown hair is a tousled mess because I've been running my fingers through it.

45

I'm not a blusher, but my cheeks are pink, and my eyes are lit up with excitement. My nipples are hard, my whole body tingling.

"Alana?" Damian asks.

I want him to moan my name. I've never fantasized about Damian before, but suddenly I want to hear him beg. I want him to plead with me to let him come, while for one night I'm the center of his world.

"Who are the other guys?" Coming back to earth, I picture the lacrosse team.

"You don't know them. They're strangers. They have no idea who you are. I just told them this would be with a friend of mine and she's cute and nice."

"I'm *nice?*"

"Well, nice enough. Trustworthy, is what I mean. And so are they. If you want this, it won't go wrong. It'll go the way you want it to."

I close my eyes. "Why are you doing this for me?"

"Your birthday's coming up."

"Not for three weeks." I'm surprised he remembers. I haven't said anything about it.

"Okay, it's your birthday month. Happy April."

I laugh. Suddenly, I feel lighter and happier than I have in awhile during this long college semester. A birthday present. Why not?

"How many, Damian?" My voice drops into a flirty tone. No, more raspy than flirty. Sex voice. It's not on purpose, it's just happening.

"Five."

"Including you?"

I hear his breathing change.

"Including me." His voice deepens.

He's aroused, and at the sound of his desire, my body responds. I stretch out on my bed, watching my reflection as I lift my T-shirt above my breasts.

"You want me to suck your cock?" I cup one breast, playing with it.

He inhales sharply. "Yes."

"It would feel so good, wouldn't it?" I slip my hand into the waistband of my leggings. "I'd take my time with you."

"I know you would."

"And I'd tease." My fingers slide into my panties, and I gasp when they meet my pussy. Fuck, so wet. So hot.

"I don't doubt it." His tone drops to a whisper. "Are you touching yourself?"

I tense up. He's not supposed to take control. But my pussy tightens around my fingers.

"Mmm-hmmmm," I murmur.

He lets out a low moan, like he doesn't mean to, but it slipped out.

"I'm playing with my pussy, Damian. You're getting me sooooo wet. I'm thinking about driving you crazy."

"Fuck," he whispers.

"It would be so much *fun* to see you naked." God, I'm trying to hold the reins, but I'm getting hungry for the sight of his body. He groans. "It would be even more fun to lick you while I'm touching your friends." His breath speeds up. "And it would be the most fun for your friends to watch —" I circle my clit faster, my thighs quivering — "when you spurt your cum in my mouth."

"Jesus, Alana!"

I drink in the sounds of him climaxing as I arch off the bed, meeting my own hand, plunging my fingers into my pussy. I'm so close, burning with excitement, but I'm not going to let myself come on the phone. I'll wait till I'm alone.

His groans are the sweetest music to my ears. I picture his hard stomach, streaked with cum, and his dick gripped in his fist. Finally, all I hear is his breath.

"I'll think about it, Damian."

I hang up before he can respond. Rolling onto my stomach, I rock against my hand, dreaming about all those cocks begging for attention. I imagine Damian's face as he orgasms. And I rub my swollen clit until I finally, finally come.

*

The next Friday night, I walk across campus to Damian's apartment. His roommate's out of town. The night is warm, but I shiver with anticipation.

I told him yes.

He said he'll take care of everything.

When I pass a window, I check my reflection. It's nothing fancy — there's no point in dressing up for tonight. I'm going to be spending a lot of time on my knees. But I look cute. My long brown hair's pulled into a ponytail, and my tank top and leggings show off my body. I'm ready to run a marathon, if that marathon involves a lot of cleavage.

At Damian's front door, I lift my hand to knock, then pause.

Behind his front door, five men are waiting. Not just five cocks; there are people attached. Maybe it was a mistake to do this sober.

Or maybe it's all an elaborate ruse on Damian's part to get me over here. The door will swing open and he'll pop out of a giant birthday cake, stripper-style.

Surprise! It's just you and me. The other guys couldn't make it. But now that you're here...

I rap firmly on the door.

Damian opens it. No one's behind him in the living room.

Instead of our usual hug, we just stare at each other. The air is thick between us.

"Are you sure about this, Alana?" he asks softly.

He looks delicious. I eye his T-shirt and jeans, his broad shoulders, his bare feet. His messy dark hair, falling over his forehead. His brown eyes, gleaming with anticipation, but also caring. He'd call this off in a heartbeat if I wanted him to.

I put my hand on his chest, and he swallows. His skin is hot through his thin cotton tee.

"Where are the other guys?"

"In my room."

"Hell, yes, I'm sure." I roll my shoulders back, aware of his eyes dropping down my body. "I'm offended you'd even ask."

"I had to." He grins. "You look amazing. Come on."

He takes my hand and pulls me toward his bedroom. I open my mouth to remind him that I'm doing the touching tonight, not being touched.

But his hand feels so nice, and what comes out instead is, "I look amazing, huh?"

"Mm-hm. Fucking hot."

I open his bedroom door.

Five guys look up at me.

Instead of sitting naked in a row, they're fully dressed and grouped around the room. They lounge on Damian's bed, his desk chair, against his dresser. Like he said, they're all strangers to me, and I don't see a flicker of recognition in any of their eyes.

What I do see is relief. Arousal. Surprise.

One guy was scrolling through his phone when I opened the door. He shoves it in his pocket and sits up straight.

"Holy shit," another one murmurs. "You're actually here. We thought Damian was shitting us. And you're hot—"

"Shh." I put a finger to my lips. He looks startled, but stops talking. The guy next to him snickers.

Damian shuts the door with a soft click.

"Let's start with some ground rules." I smile at all of them. Five pairs of eyes stare back. They're already mentally undressing me. Imagining how my mouth will feel. The guy in the desk chair shifts, and my gaze drops to the bulge in his pants. "No speaking unless you're spoken to. No touching me unless you're invited to. Is that clear?"

"Wow," begins the guy closest to me, "you are *really* into control—"

"*Sshhh*," everyone else hisses.

Good. They get the idea.

I walk over to the guy who spoke, the one who was nervous about me wanting control. He's good-looking — black hair, blue eyes, big muscular body. I put my hands on his shoulders, stroking them, and excitement floods my skin as he stares up at me. Fuck, this really is like being in a candy store. Straddling him, I lean in for a kiss.

He's surprised. Probably expected me to go straight for his crotch. But he kisses me back, running his hands over my back and pulling me onto his lap. It feels delicious, and I can't resist rubbing my pussy against his very hard erection. Around us, the other guys are fidgeting. Adjusting themselves. Breathing faster.

His kisses are getting more aggressive, with lots of tongue. His hands are roaming everywhere. My face, my arms, my breasts. I break the kiss.

"What's your name?" I murmur, brushing my lips against his ear.

"Anthony."

Anthony is used to being in control. He needs a reminder of who's in charge.

"What's yours?" he asks. I shake my head.

"Hands behind your back, Anthony."

He stares at me. I nod and give him an encouraging smile. Slowly, he puts his hands behind his back, gripping them together. I reward him by brushing my hard nipples against his chest. He groans softly. As I tease him, stroking his skin, slipping my hands under his shirt, brushing my fingers against the thick bulge in his pants, every breath and gasp he takes are echoed by the other guys in the room.

I drop to my knees, keeping my hands on his legs.

"I can't wait to taste you," I murmur. "Take your clothes off."

It's a funny thing, giving orders while kneeling. But as Anthony looms over me, hastily stripping off his shirt, jeans, and boxers, there's no doubt now about who's in charge.

His cock springs free. It's everything I want: thick, veined, flushed with arousal. A bead of precum glistens at the tip.

"Mmmmm." I smile up at him.

When I glance over my shoulder, the force of four other male stares almost knocks me over. All that concentrated desire, all that need...

"Strip," I order. "All of you. I want to see you naked."

I'm too impatient, too excited, to wait for each of them to undress when I get to them. I want a roomful of bare-assed guys, riveted to me and wondering if I'll take my clothes off too.

Some of them leap to their feet. Others stay seated as they

yank off their shirts. But they're all in a rush, eager to expose themselves.

Anthony clears his throat, angling for my attention. It turns into a groan as I stroke his thighs, ignoring his obvious need. He can wait while I take in the vision of his friends throwing their clothes off. So many guy clothes — T-shirts and hoodies and pants and boxers, all flying onto the floor. So many hard bodies. Hungry cocks.

Damian's bedroom already smells like sex and it's soaked in desire. My panties are fucking wet. I let out a moan, even though I don't mean to.

Then I turn back to Anthony. Gripping his cock, I engulf it in my mouth.

"Fuuuuuck," he hisses.

The shock of the first contact ripples through the room. He's so thick and hard as my lips wrap around him. I swirl my tongue over his head, wanting to bring him off fast. He tries to fuck my mouth, and I squeeze his shaft so I can stay in control.

Out of the corner of my eye, the other guys are staring. Their lips part as they slowly rub their cocks.

The only one I can't see is Damian. He's out of my line of vision. And dammit, I so want to see him. Is he touching himself or holding back? Is he smiling, or is his familiar face clouded with lust?

I focus on Anthony. He's close. Flexing, breathing rapidly, his hands fisting behind his back. I suck his head faster, fondling his sensitive balls, coaxing him to give me his climax.

I look up into blue eyes. *Come on, Anthony.*

"Jesus!" It comes out as a shout. His deep grunt echoes through the room, and the other guys make noises in sympathy. Curses, groans.

Hot cum floods my mouth, and I hold his gaze while I swallow. I want him to know how much I enjoy it.

Anthony collapses back on the bed, grinning like an idiot.

Quickly, I pivot to the guy next to him, the talkative one who thought Damian was shitting all of them about this evening. I don't ask his name. I don't make fucking conversation. I just start kissing his chest. Soft little kisses, and nibbles, and a bite on his nipple that makes him yelp.

"Don't you want to know my name?" he asks.

"Uh-uh." I tease his hard abs with my tongue.

"Don't you want to take this off?" He runs his fingers under the straps of my tank top. I shiver, goosebumps speckling my skin, but I push his hand away.

"Not right now."

"Don't you want to—"

I put my finger to his lips. "Quiet. Or I'll have to hush you up."

Laughter runs around the room, quick and charged.

"I'd like to see that," says the guy lounging against the dresser. He watches me through slitted eyes. "It's more than any of us can do."

Damian shoots him a look, and he subsides.

I kiss a trail down to Talkative Boy's crotch. He's silent now. But when I take his bare cock in my hands and begin to caress his warm skin, he can't hold back. All the *fucks* and *christs* and *oh shits* come pouring out. And when I think of Damian watching me get his friend off, I suck relentlessly, encouraging his orgasm with my hands and mouth.

Why can't I see Damian? Is he deliberately staying out of my sightline? Teasing me back?

The other guys are close; Anthony and a blond guy with

glasses are practically on top of us, and the guy lounging by the dresser watches with a slight smile as he slowly fists his dick.

It would all be perfect if I could just see Damian's face.

A string of curses rips through the air as Talkative Boy spurts onto my tongue. I lick his cock through his climax, eager for every drop, savoring the way his mouth hangs open when I swallow his cum too.

As he sprawls on the bed to recover, I grab the hands of the blond with the glasses, pull him to his feet, and push him against the opposite wall. He's caught off-guard, which is fun. Excited as hell, which is even better. But I also do it because I want to see Damian at the same time.

Finally, I can look him over. He's leaning against the wall, his strong arms folded. His body is beautiful, and his cock's as aroused as everyone else's. But he isn't touching himself like the others. He's just waiting. Watching me. Like a hawk.

I get the feeling he can wait a long time. Outlast all the teasing I can dream up.

I flush down my chest. I'm the one off-balance now. With a deep breath, I unhook the blond's glasses, set them on Damian's desk, and pull him in for a kiss.

His hands flex in the air. He's obviously unsure whether he can touch me. I haven't given him an order the way I did for Anthony. I let him wonder as I suck on his neck and throat. There's no doubt I'm leaving hickeys, little remembrances of this night. He doesn't offer a word of protest.

The room is truly silent now, soaked in sex. I know without looking that the guys who already came are getting hard again.

I drop to my knees and close my eyes, letting sensation take over. This boy's musky scent, his satiny skin. When I tease the underside of his cock with my tongue, his hands suddenly slide into my hair.

The room takes a breath.

I don't shake him off or tell him no. I let him massage my scalp, loosening my ponytail, just because it feels so damn good. When he holds the back of my head while I suck his cock, I let out a little sigh.

Suddenly, there's the warmth of a body close to mine. Someone's crouching next to me. I feel a hand on my back, and I know from his scent that it's Damian.

He rubs slow circles over my tank top, and all I can do is shiver with pleasure. I was excited before, but my nipples are achingly hard now, and my pussy's soaked from his simple touches.

As I focus on his friend, taking his cock deeper in my mouth, I gasp at the sensation of a warm palm fondling my breast. Damian — no, not Damian. Both his hands are on my back now, roaming from my shoulders to my waist. Unfamiliar hands are stroking my body, and I don't want to open my eyes to see who it is. I'm slipping from my perch of power. Dangerously aroused, even nervous.

I tense up.

"Do you want us to touch you?" Damian gently strokes my ass.

I moan around the blond's cock, hesitating in my answer. Finally, I open my eyes to meet his, wide with need, then those of the guy who was leaning against the dresser, which are narrowed with arousal. He's the one playing with my breast. Kneeling next to me, with Damian behind me.

"Do you want me and Thomas to touch you?" Damian repeats.

Fuck it, being touched doesn't have to mean giving up

control. I'm still driving them crazy.

I nod. Then I squirm as Thomas slides both hands over my breasts to pinch my nipples through my tank top. They respond instantly to his touch, puckering and tingling. I'm aware of the circle of guys tightening. Anthony and Talkative Boy climbing off the bed, crowding on the floor behind me, Damian and Thomas hemming me in, the blond trying to thrust into my mouth as I take him in deeper.

"Do you want us to take your clothes off?" Damian traces a finger along the small of my back. I quiver, and he tugs lightly on the waistband of my leggings. "Tell us, baby."

Where is he getting the nerve? He knows my fantasy. I'm in charge. *Baby.* I never thought I'd hear that from Damian.

But my body is shaking with excitement. Like it has a mind of its own, my ass tilts toward him, inviting his touch. I nod as I lick and suck.

Damian hooks his thumbs into my leggings and panties, easing them slowly down my ass. I shiver as another hand tentatively strokes my curves. I'm so wet, and they can see it now as Damian pulls my soaked panties down to my knees. My flushed pussy peeks from between my thighs.

Someone groans.

"So beautiful, Alana," Damian murmurs.

Alana.

Dammit, he wasn't supposed to say my name. Not right now.

"Alana?" Thomas tweaks my nipple. "So that's your name. Pretty."

"Quiet," I order.

But wasn't that what I'd hoped for? To hear Damian moan my name, his voice loaded with excitement?

God, his touch is completely unhurried. He caresses my clit lightly, his other hand playing with the opening to my cunt, while Thomas squeezes my breast and pinches my nipple, rough and excited.

"You're so wet," Damian murmurs, and he sounds...proud. "God, Alana. You're so. Fucking. Wet."

All I can do is make soft noises of excitement, because my mouth is stuffed full of cock.

"Everyone here wants to see you come. Do you want that?" He works a finger into me, and I let out a muffled cry. The blond boy's cock slides deeper into my mouth, and he curses softly. I try to focus on his pleasure — fondling his balls, swirling my tongue over his shaft. Thomas eases down my tank top and bra cup together and takes my nipple into his mouth, sucking and biting. My senses are started to flood.

"Mmmph." I nod.

"Do you want to be fucked? Do you want me to fuck you after I make you come?"

Need is taking over as I let go of control. I'm in a haze of desire, about to slip over the edge. I push against Damian, rubbing my cunt emphatically against his hand.

He grasps my hips. "Say it. Take your mouth off Michael's cock and tell me what you want."

Michael. So that's his name.

I stop sucking. Michael has his hands buried in my hair, and when I look up at him, his face is twisted in an expression of pained ecstasy — some combination of *please fuck him* and *please don't stop.*

"I want to strip," I manage.

I tear off my tank top and toss my bra aside so I'm as naked as the guys. I feel a surge of power as they drink my body in, followed by a surge of pleasure when Thomas squeezes my bare breasts.

"Fuck!" The blond guy, Michael, explodes as I keep jacking him, staring at my naked chest and his friend's hands on my breasts. The first spurt catches me on the lips. Instead of taking him in my mouth, I aim his cock downward, letting him cum all over my cleavage. Something tells me that's exactly what he needs right now. Thomas catches on quickly, lifting my breasts and moving his hands to expose my nipples. I moan when hot cum runs over them.

In a daze, I beckon to Thomas to stand in front of me. God, I want everything that Damian is offering, but if I let go now, I'll never finish what I came for.

Damian never stops touching me as I cup warm, heavy balls in my hands. Never stops rubbing my soaked folds as I open my mouth and let a new cock slide over my tongue.

Thomas grips my hair firmly. I welcome his roughness. It anchors me as the floor threatens to drop out.

Men's hands roam all over me, but only Damian's are busy between my legs. I open my mouth wider as it's filled with cock, lick and suck frantically, let Thomas's head nudge my throat. He's thick and hot and I bury my nose in his dark thatch of hair.

"Fuck, that's good, Alana," Thomas croons, pulling my hair hard. Dammit, he knows hearing my name from him is throwing me off-balance, and he's doing it deliberately. "You look beautiful like this. I have so much cum for you."

He's close. I'm close. We're all so fucking close. I pull off Thomas, just for a second.

"Damian…" God, I'm the one moaning his name, pleading for his touch. "Make me come. Fuck me."

Then I close my eyes and surrender.

It all happens quickly. Damian's fingers twist inside me as he circles my swollen clit. Thomas's cock fills my mouth, over and over. More hot male hands, all the other guys, explore my curves — my ass, my hips, my breasts, even my throat.

I shudder. I can't hold it together any longer.

And I'm not alone.

I'm with Damian.

And a whole crowd of his friends.

I explode in the most intense orgasm of my life.

As it ebbs, there's too much sensation for me to distinguish who's where. But I know it's Damian's cock sinking into me from behind, hard and excited and so pleasurable it's almost painful. It's Damian who's fucking me deeper and deeper as Thomas groans and spurts onto my tongue and a thicket of hands rove over my sweaty skin.

When Damian comes, I realize everyone else has pulled back. It's just him and me, with his hands planted on my hips and my fingers gripping his rug. His orgasm echoes through my body, and the last thing he says is my name.

Finally, he withdraws. A circle of guys stares at us: exhausted, satisfied, grinning, dazed.

I look over my shoulder and beckon to Damian.

"Come here," I rasp. "I'm not done with you yet."

He has the biggest smile on his face as he kneels in front of me. I've never seen him so happy — or been so happy myself.

All eyes are on me as I lick my juices off Damian's cock. Someone utters an awed curse. When I've lapped up every drop, I slump to the floor with my head in his lap, a sweaty mess of sex and heat.

In time, the other guys clean up and leave. Before they go, they all crouch down to say *thank you* and *that was amazing* and *you were incredible.* They part ways with a kiss on my forehead or a touch on my back. Because they're respectful like that.

When the apartment is empty, Damian and I get in the shower. It's quiet at first. We splash each other with water, do a little awkward joking around with the soap. Then we meet each other's eyes and start laughing.

"You were so hot." He runs his fingers through my wet hair. "Alana, you were fucking unbelievable."

I move behind him and reach around to rub his firm chest with soapsuds. "No, you were. Did you set all this up just to get with me?"

"It might have crossed my mind." He gives me an impish kiss over his shoulder. "You okay with tonight being different than your fantasy...*baby?*"

"Different was SO much better." I press my forehead against his back. "Sure, it's hot to imagine blowing eighteen guys in a locker room, but—"

"Eighteen?" Damian twists to stare at me.

"Or, you know, however many guys are on your team."

He leans against the shower wall, shaking with laughter. "Try fifty."

"Fifty?" I gape.

"You've never bothered to come to a game, have you? Never watched me. Never fact-checked your own fantasy."

"All right! I'll come, I'll cheer for you. And tonight was infinitely better than giving head to fifty guys. But I never gave *you* an actual blow job. We'll have to fix that...soon."

I draw a line with my wet fingertip over his abs, tickling his belly button. He turns around and catches my hands.

"I didn't think you'd ever see me this way."

"What way?"

"As a guy. As more than a friend."

"I do now." I hug him tight and rest my head on his shoulder. Slowly, his arms come up to surround me. As if, even after everything we did tonight, he can't believe this is truly happening. "Look, I don't really date, but I want to do more-than-friend things with you. A lot more."

"Good," he murmurs. "Because I do too."

"Are you sure? Do you have any idea what you're in for?"

He grins. "After tonight, I have a few ideas. Do you know what you're in for, Alana?"

I look at his familiar face, his dark curls slicked back with water. And I realize that I don't know. I have no fucking clue what I'm in for with Damian.

All I know is that he's full of surprises.

"I'm in for all of you." I pull his head down for a kiss. "I want all the things you are."

DISTURBING THE PEACE

This silent retreat is killing me.

A week on the rocky coast sounded perfect. No stress, no distractions. Just trees and shrubs and people looking for inner peace.

But I didn't count on the sitting still part. Or the noise in my head that's louder than anything in the outside world.

I'm sitting in a room with forty other people, all kneeling on mats on the wooden floor. We're two days in, and during the first meditation session, there were plenty of sounds as people got settled. But everyone else seems to have found their stride.

I'm no good at sitting still. And I'm definitely not the silent type. I came here because I needed a break from life, but life keeps chasing me.

I shift on the mat to peek out the window. Pine trees rustle, moving freely in the wind. When I tear my gaze away, I catch an annoyed glance.

It's him.

Again.

Every time I fidget or yawn, this one jerk gives me a disapproving look. Which just makes me fidget more. We're supposed to keep our gazes cast down, but whenever I see him,

I'm increasingly on edge.

My long curly red hair falls into my face, tickling my cheeks. I quickly twist it into a bun and catch him watching me with narrowed eyes, as if he can't meditate with all that distraction.

I cough. He glares. I'm not sure which one of us is less peaceful right now.

And to make it worse, he's hot. Disturbingly so.

Dark hair, dark brows, olive skin, startling blue eyes... I don't trust hot guys.

When he turns away, I check him out. We're supposed to dress modestly here. But even with his loose white T-shirt and pants, there's enough bronzed skin on display to give me an idea of his body — a dirty idea.

He's thirty-something, like me. No wedding ring. His hands are beautiful. Of course they are.

I try to stay calm and ignore him. But during the walking meditation, I trip and lose my balance. During mealtime, I drop a dish. Each time, he shoots me a *look*, as if I'm messing up his whole day.

After lunch, I exit through the wrong door. Naturally, he's rounding a clump of scraggly pines, probably coming back from the restroom, and I accidentally brush past him.

My bare arm presses against his with a sudden shock. My pale freckled skin makes a startling contrast to his bronzed forearm. His blue eyes open wide, and for a second, neither of us moves.

Our eyes lock. We say nothing, of course. But the touch, the eye contact — these are all against the rules.

I'm suddenly, completely aware that my breast is nudging his arm. My nipple's so hard that it aches. My gaze drops to his loose pants, and I stare at the tent of his erection before dragging my eyes back to his flushed face.

On cue, we both jump back. He rakes a hand through his hair and gives me that look of pure annoyance. All my nerves are wide awake. On edge, I let out a giggle and get another glare. I stick my tongue out at his sexy back, and dammit, he turns and sees. Hurrying away from his disapproval, I bite down more laughter.

But underneath, I'm ruffled. Pissed off. His attitude is ruining my retreat.

Not to mention his warm body, which I imagine pressing into mine for the rest of the day. Brushing my nipples, teasing my breasts.

But I want more than a tease from him. I want weight and force. I want him to *make* me be still. Pin me down, order me with those blue eyes to focus. And when I do, he rewards me by spreading my legs to discover how wet I am…

That night, I touch myself in bed. It's against the rules; we're supposed to be celibate throughout the retreat. But it's the only way I know how to calm down right now.

I feel him on top of me, massaging my soaked pussy. He dips his head to suck my nipple into his mouth. Kissing me hard, invading me with his tongue. He grips my curls in his fist and sinks his cock into my tightness, fucking me deeper and deeper until I don't break focus for an instant.

He's everywhere, on me and inside me. I shudder and squeeze my thighs around my hand, rubbing my sensitive clit until I come in a rush.

The next day, I'm calmer. I fidget less when we're sitting, and I don't lift my gaze to scan the room for him.

In the afternoon meditation session, I close my eyes and breathe deeply. I can smell the pines outside, the scent of sun-baked dirt and needles.

The swirling thoughts slow down. Finally, I find a measure of peace. Time hangs suspended until the ping of the brass meditation bell.

But when I resurface, heat washes over me. My eyes pop open, and as if pulled by a magnet, I turn. To look at *him*.

He's staring at me, caught out in the moment, and for once he isn't glaring. There's a look of such raw longing on his face that I feel it through my whole body.

Right now, he's not some disapproving guy. He's naked, vulnerable. Carrying a heavy load. Something drove him here, and he doesn't know whether to escape it or deal with it.

I look away quickly, trying to return to the peace, but all I can think about is him.

That night after lights-out, I tiptoe down the hall until I spot a door that's ajar. Somehow, I know.

I push it open just far enough to see him sitting on his bed. The window's open, and moonlight illuminates his beautiful face and body. He's shirtless.

His face changes when he sees me.

"You," he whispers.

The shock of hearing someone speak for the first time in three days — of hearing *his* deep voice — tightens my body. I go to him, more boldly than I would approach a stranger in the outside world, and put my finger to his lips.

He catches my hand in both of his. "You're driving me crazy."

"Sshhh." I cup his cheek and gasp when he licks my palm.

Pulled in by mindless attraction, I straddle this stranger and perch on his thighs. I stroke his broad back and shoulders, daring to suck on his neck. His skin is so warm. Salty.

He sinks his fingers into my curls, his touch unbelievably pleasurable, then twists my hair harder and harder, encouraged by my quickening breath, until I let out a little cry.

When he kisses my lips, it's sudden and taking. Quick, short, rough kisses, hard and abrupt. I've never been kissed like that. I shiver, sinking down on his lap until I nudge the large bulge in his shorts.

"You're so hot," he pants between kisses. "You're so irritating. I can't think—"

"Ssh, ssh, shh," I soothe, sliding my hands over the heat of his bare chest. I won't let him goad me into talking.

He groans when I stroke his nipples. I crouch to taste one, swirling my tongue over the tiny hard nub. His fist tightens in my hair.

"I want to see you," he whispers. "I want to see your body."

I straighten, lift the hem of my nightgown to my waist, and nod at him in the moonlight. He gets the hint, pulling the sheer fabric quickly over my head.

"Beautiful," he hisses, staring at my freckled shoulders, my breasts, the smooth expanse of my stomach.

In a second, my breasts are in his hands. I stifle my whimpers on his hard shoulder as he squeezes and caresses the soft curves, pinching my puffy nipples until tears spring to my eyes.

"Tell me what you want." He lifts my chin in his hand. His dark hair falls over his forehead, his face half-shadowed in the moonlight. "Talk to me."

I pull his palm back to my breast and clasp it tightly, thrusting my yielding flesh into his grasp, letting him know that I want more force. When he responds, I hug him tight, biting my lip to keep quiet.

"I'm going to make you scream." His whisper jerks my head up from his shoulder. "I know you've been dying to. You can't help but make noise."

I shake my head firmly and kiss his mouth before he can tempt me with more words. All I'm wearing are my panties, and they're soaked with excitement. I grind against the thick stem of his cock, shaking with arousal, hoping that I'm getting his shorts wet too.

He breaks the kiss forcefully, which just gets me more excited.

"Lie down." It's meant as an order, but it comes out a plea. His deep voice cracks.

Instead, I trail kisses over his jaw and stroke the firm planes of his back. As much as I want his force, I also want to take care of him. He shudders under my touch and groans when my hand slides down the front of his shorts to cup his hard, hard cock.

I barely have the chance to give him a squeeze before my wrists are caught in his grip. When I make a noise of excitement, he groans again.

"Lie down, baby," he repeats softly.

He needs me to. I see that longing on his face, and it twines around my body, binding me close. I'm aroused and nervous because I'm suddenly very aware that this man is a stranger, and what exactly does he want to do with me?

There's some demon he's fighting, and it's brought us together in this room. Naked, or nearly so.

But I picture him on top, giving me all his weight and force, and shiver with need. Scrambling off his lap, I stretch out on the narrow bed.

In one quick tug, my panties are off. His blue eyes widen in the darkness, staring between my legs. He pulls my thighs apart, stroking my puffy lips, and spreads them to expose my throbbing pussy.

A giggle of pure excitement escapes me. Instead of glaring, his face darkens with lust.

"You're soaked." Each word that breaks the rule of silence is a tiny arrow piercing my body. "I've been wanting to taste you since the first day. Let's see how quiet you can be."

He buries his face in my pussy.

I bite his pillow as he licks my tender flesh. His shoulders shake. The emotion coming at me is as overwhelming as his lips on my clit and his tongue in my cunt. I bury my fingers in his dark hair and close my thighs around his head, holding him while he undoes me.

As he takes me to the edge, I have to moan. Little, soft, panting moans while he sucks on my clit and teases my entrance with those beautiful fingers. He seems to understand how good it feels to have my opening massaged without being penetrated. How, even though I'm holding him close, I'm self-conscious about being eaten, and I tremble under the intensity of his mouth.

Just before I spill over into orgasm, he stops.

I reach up to him, my eyes pleading, barely catching myself before I beg out loud. He smiles.

"There's something I want to do before you come." He brushes his mouth over mine, sharing my juices. "Since it's so hard for you to keep still."

Standing abruptly, he goes to his closet. The rooms here are bare, and he has only a few clothes hung up. Taking out a robe, he pulls the sash free of its loops and stares at it for a minute in silence.

He comes to the bed and kneels above me, trailing the tip of the sash over my sensitized skin. I gasp when he pushes the fabric against my pussy, rubbing my lips and clit.

"Can I tie you up, baby?" His voice is low and throaty. "Shake your head if you don't want me to."

That sash in his hand is more than simple fun and games. It means something to him. An ex-girlfriend? Ex-wife? The demon he's exorcising? God, I don't know this man at all, not even his name, and yet I'm trusting him, naked and close to coming.

I look up into his blue eyes, gleaming in the moonlight, and thread my fingers through his hair. He crouches over me, stroking my curves.

"We don't have to," he reassures me. "It's enough to touch you…to taste you."

God, I want him. I want to see what it means to him when he uses that sash. Taking comfort that there are people in the rooms on either side, I lift my arms above my head, cross my wrists, and give him a nod.

He exhales and swiftly lashes my wrists to the bed. I feel so vulnerable as he runs his hands over my body, feeling me at his leisure. All my nerves are heightened, making it harder to keep quiet. Harder to stay still. When he rolls my puckered nipples between his fingers, I cry out and bury my face in the pillow.

I hear his soft sounds of satisfaction at being in control now. His hot hands open my thighs with more force; his firm licks on my pussy are more dominating. More invasive. Less raw and emotional. But I know that control is fragile. An illusion.

I shudder under his relentless attention, shaking uncontrollably. It's clear that he finds my vulnerability deeply arousing, even comforting, because he can imagine he's in charge. When he lifts his head, his face soaked with lust and my juices, I want to strip bare for him, peel back every layer of us both. I'm so close to babbling, begging for his name, telling him mine, asking for all the words.

So I bite my lip hard as he strips off his black boxers and his gorgeous cock springs free, thick and flushed. He strokes it, pointing it at my aching pussy.

"Don't you want to come?" he asks harshly. "You're shaking, you can't even hold still for me. Beg for it."

I arch my hips, thrusting my pussy shamelessly toward him, pleading with every muscle in my body.

He smiles grimly, then bends closer, cradling my face in his warm hands, playing nice now. His cock nudges my clit, and I gasp.

"Come on, baby." His tone softens. "Come on, beautiful girl. You can have the biggest orgasm." I whimper, and satisfaction flashes in his eyes. "I know how much your little pussy needs it. All you have to do is ask."

On the surface, it's cruel. He's trying to break down my boundaries, to win. But something deeper is going on, and I'm compelled to dig in my heels and not give in. To change the course of whatever he's playing out.

A tear rolls down my cheek, squeezed out by the sheer intensity of the situation. He growls and laps it up like he's in the desert, thirsting for that single drop.

Tugging at the sash on my wrists, I give him an inch of concession.

Please.

I shape the word silently with my lips.

It's enough. He groans and dives between my legs. I can't keep back my moans as he licks every sensitive crevice. When his mouth surrounds my clit, sucking the little nub, my orgasm takes me over suddenly, by surprise. I spasm and shake, closing my thighs hard around his head.

He doesn't stop. He keeps tonguing my clit, gripping my ass to hold me to his face. I'm so wet, dripping juices onto his bed, and I can't stop coming. He growls into my crotch, reveling in my helplessness, as my hips rise off the bed and I buck uncontrollably.

I'm about to fly apart, but he's holding me together.

My noises turn pleading.

Finally, he lifts his head, and a shock passes between us.

"Do you want me inside you?" He's deliberate, controlled, but his arms are shaking.

Yes, I want to shout.

I hold his gaze for a full minute. He stops moving. Everything stops moving. Then I give him a single nod.

He exhales in a rush, and warm, hard flesh presses against my cunt. I lift my hips, and in an instant, his cock sinks into my tightness. He's big and heavy, and I gasp at being suddenly filled so completely. But my pussy's so slick and hot that it welcomes him in.

I want to clutch him to me, but my hands are bound. So I lock my legs around his strong back as he fucks me deeper and deeper.

He's babbling, like he'll die if he doesn't talk. *You're so incredible. So wet, so hot. I want to fuck you forever.*

I shudder as he unleashes an onslaught of fierce thrusts, pushing my knees to my chest, fucking out whatever ghosts are inside him. Piercing me again and again with his thick cock and the arrows of his words.

As I grip him with my cunt, straining at my bonds, I manage to capture his lips. I kiss him long and hard, our tongues tangling. Finally, he jerks away and stares.

"It's you," he whispers, looking stunned. Seeing the woman in front of him and not a ghost.

I nod and tug at the sash on my wrists, pleading with my eyes for him to release me. Swiftly, he undoes the knot. When I slide my hands up his back, over his muscled ass, into his hair, he groans. He's so close, and God, so deep, hitting the back of my pussy with savage plunges. My breasts press against his hard chest, and my world narrows down to the ferocious pleasure of being fucked by this man.

His blue eyes open wide as he shudders, thrusts, and comes deep inside me. With each spurt, he groans and grips my hair, drinking in my moans. He never looks away from my face.

Finally, he rolls off me, panting, and I curl up in his arms. As our pounding hearts slow, he kisses the top of my head, and I press my lips against his shoulder. I know what he's found. For the time being, I've found it too.

Peace.

Shortly before dawn, I stir awake. We're folded together on his narrow bed. Wake-up time is coming soon, and I need to slip back to my room before the others rise.

I inhale the spicy scent of his warm skin, brushing dark hair off his forehead, and his eyes blink open. He smiles sleepily and gives me a good-morning kiss. I point to the bedside clock and he nods.

This is the moment for me to make a graceful exit. To observe the rules for the rest of the retreat, because we've both gotten what we need. But his arms are still wrapped around me, and I don't want to let go.

Pulling back, I run my finger along his forearm and trace letters to form a word. He raises his eyebrows, but he follows along.

TONIGHT

I add the question mark with my eyes. He thinks it over and nods.

A smile tugs at his lips as he traces an answering word on my stomach. It tickles. I shiver, trying to focus on the shapes.

DANIEL

His name. I realize that by giving me that, he's making this real. What happened here is between him and me and no one else. He's dropped his baggage. It might still be in the room, but he's not carrying it.

I hesitate before replying. There's something about anonymity that's appealing. But there's no going back — only forward.

On his arm, I write *JOCELYN*.

His eyebrows lift, and I can hear his deep voice saying *beautiful*.

Before I rise, he twines one of my red curls around his finger.

I put my simple clothes on and look back at him one more time. He's sprawled on the bed, relaxed and at ease. A different man.

There's peace in this silence.

We both smile. I tiptoe out and walk into the moment before dawn.

TEACH ME

Mia fidgeted with her cosmo in the crowded London bar. Tonight, she would meet him.

Him.

The older man she'd been texting for a week.

The man who'd kept her awake at night and distracted during the day.

The man with the roguish smile, the witty banter, and the dirty mind.

Quickly, she opened the dating app on her phone and swiped to Aaron. His photo was taken from the side. He grinned rakishly at the camera, his sandy blond hair falling in his face. He was forty, fit, handsome — close to twenty years older than her.

And he made her delirious with excitement.

She glanced around. People jostled her on either side, rubbing elbows, but they were too drunk and noisy to pay any attention. Hiding her phone inside her fuzzy jacket, she found the video she'd watched so many times, she'd practically worn out the screen: a beautiful cock, flushed with arousal, the skin tight and shiny, gripped in its owner's fist. That fist shamelessly jacked it, becoming a blur, until creamy cum spurted out, flying all over the big male hand.

Mia's mouth watered, and her pussy buzzed insistently. With the text that followed the video — *kneel between my legs and clean me up, baby girl* — she'd stroked herself to a frantic orgasm. Countless times. God, he was delicious.

"Aaron," she murmured, scanning the bar. Her nipples tightened and her whole body flamed at the prospect of finally meeting him. Seeing him, hearing his voice.

Touching him.

At first, they'd just chatted. The subjects ranged from philosophy to their favorite bands to embarrassing childhood stories. He'd made her laugh out loud. Snorting tea out her nose in a cafe, in fact.

Then she got up the courage to confess four things:

She'd always wanted to be with an older man.

She was shy.

She was kinky.

She wanted to be taught.

And he drank it up. Always respectful, always making sure she was willing, but filthier by the day. He led her down a rabbit hole that started with dirty talk.

Pictures followed. *You have the most beautiful tits, little girl. So big and firm, your pink nipples begging for my tongue.*

Then came the videos. He coaxed her to hold her phone close to her slick pussy and stroke her swollen clit for him until she exploded in a flash of pleasure.

Mia loved the coaxing. She loved yielding to him, following his increasingly dirty orders. In the end, what took her over the edge in that video was knowing how much she pleased him.

God, she was wet. She squirmed on the barstool. They'd agreed to just talk at this first meeting. Get to know each other.

Aaron had assured her he didn't expect anything.

What if I want you to expect something? she'd teased.

She smoothed her long dark hair, streaked with purple, and glanced down. Under her jacket, a low-cut black shirt showed her generous cleavage. Her short plaid skirt rode up her thighs, encased in black tights, as she scuffed one sneaker against the other.

Six months ago, she'd only dreamed of dressing like this. As she'd confided in Aaron, she'd come to London to try to break out of her shell.

Mia took a gulp of her cosmo. She'd been careful not to share identifying details, but she'd shared just about everything else. Now, she wondered if he was really who he said he was. He seemed too good to be true.

A sandy blond head in the doorway caught her attention. Her heart rose into her throat.

This was it. The meeting might be a total flop. She stuffed her phone in her purse and clasped her hands together.

Please, she prayed to whoever was listening, *let this be goddamn perfect.*

She started across the room, her pulse skyrocketing. That was definitely Aaron walking into the bar. He looked around calmly. Confidently. Unbuttoning his coat.

She'd worried that he wouldn't look like his picture. That even the videos lied. But as she approached him, it was clear that the man in front of her was no lie.

For a second, she thought about running. Not because she didn't want him, but because she wanted him so much. They'd connected so easily over text. She'd told him things — *shown* him things — no one else could even guess.

She stopped in front of him. When his warm brown eyes met

hers, her throat closed up.

Dammit, don't be shy now. He's seen you naked.

He tucked a strand of purple-streaked hair behind her ear, and her cheeks burned. The simple gesture made it hard to breathe.

"Hi," she managed. "It's me."

He flashed an impish smile, showing the dimple in his square chin. "You."

Along with the smile, there was a strange tickle of recognition that she couldn't place.

She stretched out her hand, and he took it.

"And it's you." Her dry throat made her voice rasp.

"None other." He surveyed her, still holding her hand, then pulled her into a hug.

It was a friendly hug. No pressure, no expectations. But her arms instinctively tightened around his neck, and her body followed.

Even through their winter coats, she felt her breasts bump his firm chest. She let out a soft noise as his hands settled on her curvy hips.

"Molly, sweet girl," he whispered.

Right. In an abundance of caution, she'd used a different name on the app, planning to tell him her real name in person if all went well.

At the time, it had seemed like a great idea.

Mia pulled back. "I have to tell you something."

"Anything." He took her chin in his hand.

Recognition pulsed, stronger. She'd met this man before, and she couldn't place where. Something shifted in his eyes, and he peered at her more closely.

"My name isn't really Molly." She fought to hold his gaze.

"It's actually Mia. I used an assumed name on the app, you know, just to be on the safe side…"

He blinked, surprised, then grinned. "All right. I'm not mad about it. Mia's a beautiful name. And I understand—"

His eyes suddenly widened, then narrowed. Her name had rung a bell. As he opened his mouth, the truth came to her too.

"Mia," he repeated. "Would that be Mia—"

"Oh my God." She put her hand to her mouth.

"Mia Hawkins?" His arms stiffened around her.

"Oh God, you're—"

He held her away from him.

"Shit," he gritted. "Shit, shit."

"Jesus," she breathed.

"You look so different. I didn't know."

She stared up at him. "Professor Taylor?"

His hands hovered over her without actually touching. She could feel the heat radiating from his palms, through her jacket, burning her soft skin.

"Modern Literature, front row," he muttered. "Great work but never participated."

"It's okay," she said quickly. "It doesn't matter, it's not a big deal. That was last year."

She never would have expected to soothe him. He was older, more experienced. But she stroked his back and cupped his cheek. His breath quickened, and he flinched.

"It's okay, Aaron," she repeated.

"No, it's not okay."

"I'm not your student anymore. We're across the ocean from the university."

"Are you still enrolled?" His voice was terse and businesslike.

Fuck it, she'd give anything for him to hold her again and call her his sweet girl.

"Yes." Her eyes dropped. "I'm doing my junior year abroad here. What about you?"

"I'm on sabbatical. Researching and writing." She stared up at him, and he swallowed. "We can't do this, Mia."

"Yes, we can."

"I pride myself on being ethical, and this is completely unethical."

Goddammit. She'd finally met a man she liked, a man she was overwhelmingly attracted to, a man she could be *herself* with, and this was over before it began?

Mia had always been a people pleaser. She hated arguing. Hated making a fuss. She kept her mouth shut, even when she had something to say.

That ended now.

She straightened her shoulders and took a deep breath. "You know what? I love you for saying that, but I also hate you for saying that."

His mouth fell open.

"What are you so afraid of? Do you think I'll get you in trouble? Is that it? 'Professor Taylor sent me dick pics?'"

"That's part of it," he muttered.

"I would never do that." The words rushed out, gathering strength. "I'm completely, totally on board with everything we've done. I would never try to hurt you. *Never.* And I know you'd never take me anywhere I don't want to go."

"All that from a week of texting?" He raised an eyebrow. His face softened, hinting at the dimple in his chin.

"We've talked a lot. I've said more to you in the past week than I have to most people in my life."

"I believe you, Mia." The dimple showed itself. "You never said a word in class last year, but you've talked my ear off the past few days. Practically broke my phone."

"No, that was you." Her cheeks flushed.

"You didn't wear makeup back then, did you?" He traced a finger over the dark lipstick on her full lips. "Your hair was much shorter. Definitely not purple. And you favored... turtlenecks."

His warm brown eyes dropped to the glimpse of cleavage, creamy and full, peeking from her fuzzy jacket. She shivered. Her nipples ached, feeling the force of his eyes through her tight shirt.

"So you can't really blame me for not recognizing you." His smile was relaxed now. Wicked. "I don't know what your excuse is. Or do you have one?"

"I swear I didn't recognize you, Aaron."

"Really."

"Really! No glasses now. Longer hair." She dared to run her fingers through the sandy blond locks. "Completely different context."

He was calm now. In control. Pinning her to the spot with his gaze, making her squirm in the most delicious way.

"You were so quiet in class, but I could tell a lot was happening under the surface. And the papers you turned in were beautiful. I don't get to read a lot of beautiful papers."

Thank you, she was about to say. What came out instead was, "I don't want to hear about my beautiful papers right now."

His eyebrows shot up.

She slipped her hands under his coat. His wool sweater was soft yet prickly under her palms. He caught her wrists in a tight grip. The suddenness made her gasp.

"Dinner first," he said firmly. "We'll talk."

"I don't want to just talk."

His hand tangled in her hair and closed in a fist. She inhaled sharply. "Brat."

"We can have dinner afterwards." Her heart beat madly, stunned at her own forwardness.

"And do what beforehand?" The hand in her hair twisted, pulling her head back, forcing her to look at him.

She hesitated.

"Tell me, baby girl." His eyes narrowed. This was the Aaron she'd come to know over the past week. Dirty, dominant, soaked in lust.

Her cheeks bloomed red. "Right here in the bar?"

"You want it, I expect you to ask for it. Explicitly." He wasn't smiling now.

Her courage was about to flee. She swallowed hard. For Aaron, she could do this.

"I want you to take me back to your place." Her voice came out a whisper. "And I want you to teach me."

He exhaled, and his eyes turned to slits. "Teach you what?"

"Everything."

"Mia…" He drew her name out in the sweetest caress. "What a little slut you are. You're even naughtier than I thought."

Her chest rose and fell, too excited to respond. She managed to squeeze out one sentence. "Does that mean you're okay with it?"

He raised his eyebrows.

"With us?" she pressed.

He surveyed her slowly. His gaze set her whole body on fire. That mischievous smile flickered over his face.

"Button your coat, sweetheart," he said. "We're going home."

He held her hand firmly as they left the bar. Mist dampened the air, and streetlamps cast pools of light in the early evening.

Mia stiffened as Aaron led her confidently down a maze of streets. God, she was trusting him completely. A week of dirty texts, a sense of safety because she'd liked him as a professor — was that enough to go on?

He squeezed her hand. "Okay, baby?"

"I'm nervous," she blurted.

"In a good way or in a bad way?"

"I'm not sure."

He stopped and took her face in his hands. "We're not going to do anything you don't want to, sweet girl. We can stop any time."

"Does that turn you on that I'm nervous?"

His eyes crinkled, and she immediately felt better. "When you're shy, absolutely. Worried, no. Are you sure about this?"

She nodded vigorously.

"Good."

"What do you like about me being shy?" she ventured, as they slowed in front of a narrow building and turned in the front gate. Her heart pounded at the thought of going into Aaron's house…stripping naked for him…

He considered her. "It's sexy to know that you have layers and you're peeling them back for me. I'm shy too."

Mia gaped at him. "Shut up. You are? I can't believe that. You seem so confident. So in control."

"Years of practice." He winked at her. "Every semester on the first day of classes, I get nervous. Have to give myself a pep talk in the mirror and run a few miles. Can't eat, can't sleep."

She eyed him suspiciously as he unlocked the front door. "You're just trying to make me feel better."

His smile made her melt. "Is it working?"

His flat was attractive: brick walls, plants in the corner, records scattered on the coffee table. The cozy mess made her feel at home. But she barely had time to take it in, because he tossed his coat on the couch, backed her against the wall and covered her mouth with his.

The kiss took everything and left her gasping.

"I know you're shy, baby." He loomed over her with a devilish smile. "But right now, I want you to undress for me."

She turned bright red. Even though she'd shown him everything on camera already.

"I want to," she blurted, "but I'm scared."

He took her face in his hands. "Mia, you asked me to teach you."

"Then help me do it."

He kissed her more softly, his lips grazing hers, as his warm hands cupped her face. Slowly, they moved down her neck, unbuttoning her jacket. When it gaped open, he slid his hands inside to rub her shoulders.

Bit by bit, Mia relaxed. The kiss became harder, deeper, more passionate. His hands moved to her collarbone. Then her neck. Then her cleavage, stroking her breasts above her low-cut shirt, slipping down every so often to graze her nipples through the clingy fabric.

Dimly, she understood what he was doing. He was getting her accustomed to his touch. Making her want more, to the point where she'd ask. Even beg.

She tore her mouth from his. It wasn't easy.

"Please." She locked eyes with him. "I — I want more."

"Mia…" he chastised. "You know better than that. Be direct. Be specific."

"Damn you, this isn't an English paper." She started to giggle.

He fixed her with a look. "Are you questioning my methods?"

"Yes, Dr. Taylor." She shook with laughter.

A grin sneaked across his face and vanished in an instant. He took her chin in a firm grip.

"Baby, if you want more, I expect you to tell me what and how. Of course, I could also just spank you until you comply."

Her laughter evaporated. "I want you to take my clothes off for me."

His voice dropped. Softer, more dangerous. "Aren't you a demanding little thing?"

The next second, her fuzzy jacket was on the floor. He pulled off her tight shirt, expertly undid her lacy bra. It was all so fast, which just added to the sudden shock of his hands on her breasts.

She was breathing so fast, she thought she'd explode.

Aaron grinned down at her. "You're turned on, aren't you? You have such luscious tits." He pinched her plump pink nipples, and she gasped. "You're blushing, Mia. I like that. All the way down to those gorgeous breasts. Touch yourself for me."

She looked down, her hair hanging in her face, as she cupped her heavy tits and lightly rubbed her thumbs over her puckered nipples.

"Good girl," he crooned, brushing the strands of purple hair away from her breasts. "Stand up straight, give me a full view."

Her chest rose and fell as she straightened, thrusting it out.

But her eyes remained downcast. She was embarrassed, but she was also fascinated, watching her own nipples get even tighter and harder, knowing Aaron was watching too...

A fist in her hair jerked her head back. His eyes were dark with lust.

"I said, stand up straight, Mia."

Her pussy throbbed with excitement. She let out a whimper. She was soaked, so soaked under her short plaid skirt.

"Yes, Aaron," she breathed.

"You know..." he mused, a smile growing on his face as he surveyed her. "You really frustrated me in class last year."

"*Me?*"

"Uh-huh." He traced her full lips with one finger. She crossed her legs, trying to seek relief from the insistent ache in her cunt. "I saw how smart you are, how brilliant and insightful, and I wished, just once, that you would open your mouth."

Her lips parted, and he pushed his finger in. She sucked on it in a rush of excitement.

"You always hid yourself." A warm hand squeezed her breast. "Your body, your mind. You kept yourself a secret. That's right, baby, keep pinching those pretty nipples for me."

She was shaking, barely able to stand.

"I tried to help you come out of your shell. Do you remember? It's all coming back to me now."

She nodded frantically.

"You'd get this look in discussions like you wanted to say something. Once I asked if you wanted to contribute. You turned bright red and shook your head."

He unzipped her short skirt. It fell around her ankles. She let out a whimper, staring up at him with glazed eyes as he fucked her mouth with his finger.

"And there was the time I called you over after class." He worked his hand inside her black tights, stroking her soft stomach. "You'd written such a strong paper, and I wanted to share it with everyone as an example."

Mia's head swirled. She remembered. He'd given her an encouraging smile. It made her feel warm inside, and she could barely look at him. She'd agreed to let him share the paper, but she'd wanted to crawl under her desk when he did.

"I hoped you'd be proud," he murmured. "You deserved to be. I want you to be proud now."

He pulled his finger from her mouth, kissed her softly, and tugged down her tights and panties together.

Instinctively she covered her pussy with her hands. God, she wanted him so much, but she was so nervous.... And, hell, hoping for that stern voice again. Maybe even a spanking.

Instead, he rubbed her shoulders, his voice reassuring. "It's okay, baby girl. I've already seen your pretty cunt, remember? I've watched you play with your sweet clit. You even spread yourself for me so I could see your tight little hole, oozing with horny juices. You were such a good girl, coming for me. And I know you're going to be a good girl for me now."

"Did it turn you on, Aaron?" she whispered, hungry to hear the answer she already knew. "Did you like seeing me touch myself?"

He chuckled softly. Dangerously. "You have no idea how many loads I shot, imagining my cum spraying all over your tender pink lips. Dripping from your little cunt after I fucked you deep."

Trembling with need, she moved her hands away from her mound, eager to show herself to him now.

"Fuck," he hissed.

Very lightly, he traced the neatly trimmed patch of dark hair and the tender skin surrounding it. She let out a whimper, and he smiled. She felt incredibly exposed, naked for him with her tights and panties around her ankles while he stood over her, fully dressed. She'd never been so excited in her life.

Gathering courage, she ran her hands over his arms and chest, exploring his body in turn. Her juices oozed down her thighs. He dragged his finger between them, collecting her cream, until he met soft bare lips.

"Oh God, Aaron, yes—"

Slowly, deliberately, he cupped her pussy and stroked his middle finger along liquid heat. When he grazed her clit, she gasped.

"So wet for me, sweet girl. I wouldn't expect anything less." He abruptly let go. "Take off those tights and panties and that skirt around your ankles. Not to mention your shoes. I want you completely naked when you walk into my bedroom."

She flushed from head to toe. Bending over, aware that he was drinking in her every move, she stepped out of her skirt and unlaced her sneakers. Her full breasts hung down, aching with need, and he was definitely staring at her ass…

"Faster, Mia." His brown eyes were hot with desire, but his voice was calm. "Otherwise I'll have to punish you and I don't want to do that on our first night."

"Oh, you don't?" Still bent over, she peeked up at him. Holding the pose now, because his attention felt good.

His mouth quirked in a grin. "Trust me, baby. I know you're eager to experience everything, but let's save something for tomorrow."

Tomorrow. The thought made her giddy. Hastily, she took off her sneakers and stripped away her tights and panties.

Aaron led her into his bedroom. She was grateful for his firm grip, because her knees were about to give out. He pushed her onto a big, soft bed and crouched over her.

"Undress me, baby," he ordered.

Eagerly, fumbling a little, she pulled his sweater over his head and ran her fingers through his sandy blond hair. It was so soft, and his lips were so close, that she instinctively pulled him down for a kiss.

Oh God, his mouth was hot, his tongue was hungry, his hands were all over her breasts like they belonged to him...

A sharp pinch on her nipple made her cry out.

He grinned down at her. "You have a job to do. Don't get distracted."

"You're nothing *but* distracting." She rolled her eyes, secretly loving the stern look he gave her. His belt came open in her hands, she tugged down his pants, and in the next minute, he loomed over her, naked.

His body was lean and hard, with just a hint of softness. In the dim light of the room, his cock curved toward her, large and beckoning.

"Hold onto the headboard," he ordered.

God, with her arms above her head, she couldn't hide anything from him. She felt incredibly vulnerable, lying beneath him while his eyes roved over her bare curves like she was a feast spread out for his pleasure.

"I've thought so much about your body, baby girl. What you'd look like, all of you." His hands followed his eyes, roaming over her arms, her stomach, her hips. He caressed her breasts, giving special attention to her puckered nipples. "Not just your beautiful tits on my screen, or even your hot little pussy coming especially for me, but all of you."

"Me too," she whispered. "You're even better in person."

"Such a naughty little girl." He opened her thighs firmly. "Mmmmm. There's the perfect pussy that's been haunting my dreams."

His finger sank inside her cunt. Her hot excitement made it easy for him to penetrate her. Still, she gasped at the invasion.

"Absolutely soaked. Spread your legs for me," he urged. "That's my girl."

She'd only had sex once. Aaron knew that. It was near the end of the one relationship she'd had. Her boyfriend had accused her of being closed off...not fun enough. Needless to say, the sex had been far from good. She'd been barely wet, clenched up tight, and it hurt.

She'd told Aaron all this. He promised her that if he ever touched her, it would be the opposite of that experience in every way.

He was right.

She moaned as he fingered her, opening like a flower under his sure attention. His thumb grazed her clit, coaxing the swollen bud into full arousal. He withdrew, and more pressure met her pussy. Bigger, thicker.

"Mia," he murmured, "you're such a good little slut for me. That's it, let me in."

She looked down. Two of his large fingers massaged her opening, pressing in.

"Is that okay, baby girl?" His voice was all soft concern, but his eyes were devouring her. "You're so fucking tight, I don't want to overwhelm your little pussy."

"Yes, yes, it's okay."

God, he felt big. She *was* overwhelmed, but in the very best way. He was going slow, exactly the way she needed.

"Aaron..." she pleaded. "I'm so close..."

"Sshhh, baby. Just feel good."

She let go of the headboard, reaching for him, and was startled by a smack on her thigh. It didn't hurt, exactly. In fact, it felt exciting with Aaron fingering her. But it did sting.

"No, Mia," he said firmly. "You'll be able to touch me later. This is about you giving me your pussy. You're going to let go and come for me and do everything I say."

Shuddering with need, she grasped the headboard.

"That's my girl." His free hand slid down from her thigh to cup her ass. A soft, tickling sensation made her squirm.

Oh my god. Her ass. He was touching her asshole, slick with her juices. Petting it, stroking it, while he probed her pussy. She squeezed down, then relaxed as he worked his finger in.

It felt so...natural for him to touch her there. So warm and good and right.

"Mia," he crooned, "you're perfect. I'm going to fill you everywhere. You're the best student I could ever hope for. I love that you're giving yourself over to me so completely. Letting me see and touch you all over. My sweet, shy little slut..."

The words swirled over her in a blissful haze. She clenched tight around his fingers, her pussy and ass together, and climaxed in a long wave. Aaron massaged her clit as she came, urging her through more ripples of pleasure. Finally she fell back to the bed and he eased his fingers out of her.

She hugged him tight, his hot flesh and hard muscles making her head spin. He kissed her, then stood.

"Kneel on the rug and wait for me."

Mia obeyed, her heart still pounding from her orgasm. She stared at Aaron's cock as he left the room. Was he going to order her to suck him? She heard the sounds of water running in the bathroom. Her pussy was hot and pulsing, and her ass tingled from his attention.

When he re-entered the room and sat down on the bed directly in front of her, she bit her lip.

"Come here, Mia," he said softly.

Quickly, she moved between his legs, riveted to the heavy, hard shaft he was stroking.

In their texts, Aaron had told her how much he enjoyed being deep-throated. And that if she wanted to learn, he'd teach her. She'd been mindless with lust as he described shooting his cum down her warm throat. She'd touched herself to his dirty words, eventually coming as she imagined his dick filling her mouth.

Of course I want to learn, she'd texted, because it had all been so hot. *I want to make you come that way.*

Now his cock was in her face, thick and veined, even more mouthwatering than on video. But Jesus, it was big. This was no fantasy. She swallowed.

"Aaron," she confessed, "I have no idea what I'm doing."

"Don't worry, baby." He stroked her hair back from her face, twisting his fingers in the purple waves. "I'm not going to give you any more than you can handle. Go at your own pace for now. Just explore."

His calm assurance excited her beyond belief. Taking a deep breath, she wrapped her fingers around his shaft. He felt wonderful, silky soft skin over rigid hardness, and it felt so right to glide her hand along his cock. She looked up at him shyly as she ran the tip of her tongue over his slit.

"Fuck," he groaned.

Gathering confidence, she swirled her tongue all over his firm head. God, he was a mouthful, but his obvious pleasure spurred her on.

She felt deliciously submissive kneeling at his feet, their positions exaggerated: the inexperienced young girl being schooled by the older man. When his grasp tightened on her hair, and his hand slid to the back of her head, she shivered in excitement.

"Good, Mia. Take me just a little deeper. You look so beautiful with my cock in your mouth. Cup my balls and play with them...fuck, yes. That's a good girl. I have so much cum for you, baby."

The craziness of it all hit her. *I'm sucking my English professor's cock.*

Breathing through her nose, she sank down on him, eagerly licking and sucking his thick shaft, until his cock slid in far enough to nudge the back of her throat.

His hands jerked, tightening on her hair in exquisitely painful pleasure.

"*Good* girl," he crooned. "Good, good girl. Relax for me, just like that."

She was unbearably excited as he fucked her mouth, slowly and surely, heaping praise on her each time he reached her throat. But there was so much of him, and she needed to catch her breath, and there was a question she just had to ask...

She pulled free, grasping his cock, and sucked in air.

"Did you want me when I was in your class?"

His nostrils flared. When he spoke, his voice was rough. "I try not to think about my students that way."

"Right," she teased. "You pride yourself on being ethical."

He gave her hair a firm yank. She felt it all the way to her toes. "The key word is *try*. And the answer is fuck, yes."

Giddy, she dove down to suck him again, worshiping the

thick flesh filling her mouth.

"I wanted to hear you talk, Mia. I wanted to know what was inside that head of yours." She sucked harder, and he hissed with pleasure. "I wanted to peel off your turtlenecks and feast on the luscious tits I knew you were hiding. I wanted to command you to suck my cock exactly the way you're doing now."

And Mia wanted him to come. She wanted to taste the cream that had spurted across her screen so enticingly. But Aaron gripped her hair and pulled her head back.

"That's enough for tonight, baby. On the bed."

She let go of his cock and gazed up at him. "How do you want me?"

He swore under his breath. "On your back."

He helped her onto the bed. Once again, he crouched over her, massaging her cunt with a sure hand. She moaned when two fingers penetrated her, easily this time. Her hands roamed over his sweaty back, his shoulders and chest, with a mind of their own.

"Fuck me, Aaron," she pleaded.

His face was dark with lust. "I'm going to, Mia. You're my gorgeous, naughty young slut and I'm going to take you here on my bed."

He pulled his fingers out of her pussy and firmly spread her thighs. As he grasped his cock, pointing it at her, she clutched his shoulders.

"I wish this were my first time."

His expression softened. "Then let's say it is. You're a sweet little virgin and I get to deflower you."

She giggled and arched up to kiss him. Then the air hissed out of her as his cock pressed against her tight cunt.

"That's right, baby. Open up for me."

Slowly, she yielded to him, her pussy clinging to his thick head.

"Aaron!" she gasped as he sank inside her.

When he began to thrust, her legs closed sharply around his back. He felt huge, but she was slick and hot and he was kissing her lips, her face, her neck, fondling her breasts, telling her how proud he was of her for taking him. It felt incredible, but—

Mia wrapped her arms around him. "I love you teaching me," she whispered. "And I want to learn from you. But right now, I just want to be us. Mia and Aaron. I'm not your student right now, I'm your—"

What was she? They'd just met. And yes, he knew most of her life story and his dick was buried halfway in her pussy, but...

He waited, crouching over her, one hand squeezing her breast. "Go ahead, Mia. I'm listening."

Maybe he did just want her to be his student. A plaything, a sweet little almost-virgin he could mold and teach.

Or maybe not.

"Your girl," she said in a rush. "Right now, I'm just your girl."

"Fuck, yes," he hissed, pulling her close.

She didn't need coaxing to take him now. When he thrust in deep, she was ready. She buried her face in his neck, licking and biting his salty skin until he groaned and ground against her clit. Her nails raked his back. Her breasts bounced with each thrust. His balls slapped her ass as he fucked her.

God, she was so full of him, so connected, and it was messy and reckless and incredibly noisy. That was the most shocking part, how much noise she was making. He was heavy and hot and hard, and as he fucked her into oblivion, his hand gripping her hair, her cries mingling with his filthy words, he gave her one order:

"Look at me."

Eyes wide, she stared up at him.

"I want to cum on you, Mia. Just like we talked about. Do you want that?"

All she could do was nod.

He pulled out. His hand blurred on his gorgeous cock. Hot cream splashed onto her breasts, her nipples, her stomach and pussy. As his cum dripped down her skin, he dove between her legs.

She gasped. He was licking up her juices with total abandon, pushing her towards another orgasm. Her need, bottled up for so long, roared through her cunt. She cried out, pushing his face into her folds, all her shyness left behind as she spasmed in a long, helpless climax.

Afterward, he held her close. As they snuggled, she traced a finger through the trail of cum between her breasts and gave it a playful lick. His brown eyes narrowed, and the mischievous grin she already loved flickered across his face.

"Since you're not my student right now, I won't tell you you're a good girl. I'll just say that was hot."

Mia laughed. "I can be your good girl too," she began, but she was cut off by the sound of his stomach...rumbling. "Are you hungry?"

He shrugged. "A certain someone said she wanted to skip dinner and go straight to my house, so I was a gentleman and obliged. And I told you what I'm like before a big event...can't eat, can't sleep...so no lunch either."

She sat up. "Wait, you were *nervous?* About meeting me?"

He stretched his arms above his head and smiled at her shock. "I didn't know what to expect, *Molly*. You can never be too careful. You seemed too good to be true."

"So did you."

He pulled her down to him. "Well, now that you've seduced me and had your way with me…" Mia rolled her eyes, a warm flush running over her body. "How about we have dinner. And talk. The way I expected this evening to go."

"Come on, Professor Taylor," she whispered in his ear. "You sent me dick pics. Are you really so surprised we ended up here?"

He tugged a handful of her hair. "Dinner. And talk. I want to listen to you, Mia. Not just read your words on paper or a screen."

For a second, she was too happy to speak.

"All right," she said finally, hugging him tight. "I think we have a lot to say to each other."

BREATH OF ANGELS

"This is our new opening act?" I stare at the man who's setting up his gear onstage.

"Kate, you know I had two hours to make this happen." Jules picks up her bass. "Pink Stink pulled out at the last minute."

"Did they come?" Mikki does a rimshot in the air.

Jules ignores her. "Don't blow a gasket, Kate."

"Oh, I'm totally okay. But him? He is not okay. Out of all the musicians in L.A., you picked this guy?"

"C'mon. He's like a sweet, non-threatening puppy."

"Exactly. Either our fans will eat him alive, or people will think they came to the wrong show and leave."

I scope out this man, who's obviously preparing for an intimate solo act. It's just him, his acoustic guitar, some type of vintage amp, and a mic. He has brown ringlets, a beard to match, and stunningly intense green eyes. But you don't get to see much of them, because they're trained on the stage as he shuffles his shoes. If it weren't for the beard, he'd look like a teenager.

"Who is he?" I demand.

"My ex-boyfriend's roommate's cousin," Jules says smugly.

"You've got to be kidding me."

"Kid you not."

"We're the motherfucking Aftershocks! He is not on-brand for us."

"Katie!" Jules squeals. She knows I hate being called that. "Since when do you talk about *brand?*"

Amanda makes a gagging noise behind us, her guitar over her shoulder. "That is so not what we're here for."

"It's not punk," Mikki puts in.

"Come *on*," Jules says. "It'll be hilarious. So maybe he'll flop. So what? He's getting exposure and we're giving our fans an ironic experience. If it comes off as a huge joke, even better."

I study him as he goes through his sound check with the house engineers. He looks earnest. Excited. Nervous. His hands shake slightly.

He's fucking beautiful. Like a poem made of flesh and nerves and hope.

I remember feeling that way before my first show at seventeen. Butterflies zooming like crazy in my belly. Fingers sweaty on the neck of my guitar, throat dry when I opened my mouth to sing.

Now I'm thirty, touring half the year with the girls.

I poke Jules. "How old is he?"

"My sources say he's twenty-three."

"What's his name?"

"Ben."

"Jules, this isn't fair to Ben. Throwing him out there to the dogs? He probably sees this as his big opportunity."

Jules searches my face for a sign that I'm joking. I stare her down.

She whistles. "Kate, I never knew you were such a

marshmallow."

Me neither. These days, I'm jaded. Indifferent to all the pretty boys and girls I got excited about when I was younger. Music is the only thing that gets me going.

"Come on." Amanda grabs my arm. "Doors open now. Let's go get dressed and see what kind of show Benjamin Bunny puts on. *We'll* cheer for him, at least."

An hour later, Ben steps in front of the mic. He's in the same well-worn T-shirt, frayed jeans, and sky-blue Chucks that he wore for the sound check. Meanwhile, the girls and I are kitted out in black, vinyl, and sass.

"Why so covered up, Kate?" Mikki wants to know, eyeing my crop top and checkered pants.

I run a hand through my shaggy pink hair and give her a quick flash of bra. "Saving the big reveal for later."

The crowd is thick and rowdy. Ben clears his throat twice before speaking.

"Hi, everyone. I'm Ben Lewis."

He's as soft-spoken onstage as off. I met him after we changed. I shook his hand, stared into those intense green eyes, and told him we were honored to share the stage with him. I hope to hell it'll be true.

"Whoo!" Amanda cheers, clapping loudly. "Yeah, Ben!"

Ben blinks and mumbles the introduction to his first song.

"We can't hear you," Mikki yells. When his cheeks flush, I whack her arm. "What?" she protests. "He needs help. He hasn't been media-trained."

"Hasn't been potty-trained, you mean," Jules chimes in, as Ben plays the opening chords. They're spare, quiet. Hauntingly beautiful. They stir me. His fingers on the strings, now steady, send ripples through the air in the club.

"Shut up, Jules," I say distractedly. "I'm trying to listen."

"Oooh, Kate."

"Kate's got a crush."

A crush? No. No, I do not have a crush. But I do have something else, something long-forgotten.

I put a hand on my bare stomach. Inside are little occupants that haven't been there in years.

Butterflies.

"Kate?"

"Oh my god, Kate."

"We've lost Kate. Call the fire department."

The audience doesn't know what to do about Ben. So they hush up. He's quiet, but intense. Earnest. Heartbreaking. With each song, he's a little more confident. He owns the stage a little more. He doesn't step fully into his presence, but the guy has talent. He's an artist. The people listening are confused as fuck, but they acknowledge that.

After the first song, I stop paying attention to the crowd, because I'm caught up in the swirl of his music. When he ends the too-short set, I have to remember to clap.

"Next show, he gets more stage time," I tell Jules.

She rolls her eyes. "If you say so, Katie."

Ben bobs his head to the applause and hurries off. Yet I still feel those long fingers making music. Tracing my tattooed shoulders and back, causing the inked flowers to bloom.

I shake it off. The Aftershocks are taking the stage, and the audience expects an inferno.

Energy crackles through the room as we set up. My back stays to the crowd until the band is ready. At Mikki's nod, I whirl to face front.

"What's up, fuckers?" I holler, slamming the mic into the

stage. Mikki explodes on the drums, and the guitars kick into overdrive.

Performing is an out-of-body experience. I'm possessed, swirling in an orgy with my bandmates. I pump energy into the crowd and it rolls back to me.

Normally, I don't pick out faces in the audience. Lines are blurred. We're all one. But this time, a single face beams from the darkness like a lighthouse.

Ben's pretty green eyes are shellshocked as he takes refuge by the merch table. He huddles near the stacks of T-shirts and CDs.

Next time I catch a glimpse, Jett at the merch table is hanging him a pair of earplugs with a shit-eating grin. Ben takes them gratefully and stuffs them in his ears.

But he doesn't flee the scene. He doesn't look away.

"We're the Aftershocks!" I yell, and the crowd roars back.

We're halfway through the set now. I'm drenched in sweat. I rip off my crop top, and the room screams at the sight of my black bra.

Thoughtlessly, I hurl the perspiration-soaked shirt straight at Ben.

His mouth opens in an O. And holy fuck, the desire to see his real O-face is suddenly so strong, it seizes me in its fist and whips me up like a milkshake.

He catches the shirt to the sound of wolf whistles. Jett claps him on the back, grinning. But Ben stands still, frozen like he's the Statue of Liberty and my shirt is the goddamn torch.

"Kate," Jules says in a low voice, her hand on my shoulder, "I think you broke Ben."

Mikki, bless her little soul, charges into an impromptu drum solo that puts everyone's attention back on the stage.

Slowly, Ben lowers the shirt. He holds it like it's a lost kitten he has no idea what to do with.

Stepping to the side to give Mikki the spotlight, I grab the bottle of Jameson on the stool by Amanda and knock back a swig.

"Be gentle with Ben," Amanda whispers. "We need him to last for the next four shows."

Jules snorts. "You think he will?"

"Well, what doesn't kill you makes you stronger." Amanda bobs her head to Mikki's solo.

We jump back into place as Mikki smashes her way to a finish and make the perfect crashlanding into our next song.

Our music is visceral. We're called the Aftershocks for a reason. It's not just about what we hit you with, it's how you feel afterward as it reverberates through your body.

I don't look at Ben in the merch corner for the rest of the night. But his gorgeous green eyes, the shock on his face when he caught my shirt, reverberate through *my* body.

The energy I put out has been tossed right back at me.

The butterflies have gone berserk.

When we close the show and I yell out our thank-yous, I point to him. Yep, still there. He's survived. And he's...sweaty. His brown curls are darkened and plastered to his forehead.

Was he dancing? Did I miss it?

"Let's all give a great big hand to Benjamin Lewis, our insanely talented opening act. He filled in on short notice and is an absolute poet. He didn't know what he was getting himself into, but now he's going to be stuck with us for the next four shows. We're so glad he's here."

Everyone cheers. Ben looks overwhelmed, but he gives a little wave to acknowledge them.

It takes awhile for the club to empty out. When it does, I slip out to the back alley for a solo smoke and find Ben there.

He's leaning against the building, one Converse-clad foot propped on the wall and his hands in the pockets of his frayed jeans. Sweat sheens his forehead. I want to run my fingers through his damp curls.

I join him and light my cigarette. For long minutes, neither of us speaks in the warm summer night.

"You were amazing," I say softly.

He laughs, but it catches in his throat. "I was terrified. *You* were amazing."

"First time playing a venue this size?"

He nods and clears his throat. "You're a singer. You shouldn't smoke."

"It gives me that raspy flavor. Mmm." I blow a smoke ring at the sky.

He's staring at me. I feel the force of his eyes from the side. "You shouldn't drink onstage either."

"Bad for my vocal chords? Or my focus?"

"Both."

"Yeah, well, you drove me to it."

"I did?" He looks so horrified that I burst out laughing and pat his shoulder.

"I'm joking. You were so shocked when I threw my shirt at you, I had to drink on your behalf. Where is it, by the way?"

"Your shirt?" An unexpected grin flits across his face. "Here."

He takes the tiny black crop top out of his back pocket. He's rolled it up neatly. Maybe he was planning on a souvenir.

I stuff it in the waistband of my checkered pants. His eyes widen adorably. Was he expecting me to put it on?

"Don't worry, Ben." Leaning against the brick wall, I thrust out my tits in their black bra. "I don't drink or smoke the way I used to. I don't fuck around the way I used to, either. This…" I gesture to the open door of the club, then to the air as music drifts from someone's apartment. "This is my drug of choice. Music. Better than sex."

He rubs a hand over his hair. "I guess." His green eyes dart down the alley and back to me. "I mean, I wouldn't know."

"You've never— Oh my God. Oh my God!" I holler. "You're a virgin?"

"Could you say it any louder?"

"I'm sorry," I say quickly, putting my hand on his arm. He blinks, and his muscles flex under my palm. "I really am. I'm just surprised, because — *you're beautiful*. I didn't mean to yell it to the skies. Can I just ask — why? You have so much going for you. You're talented and sweet." The sincerity in my voice surprises me. "Don't get me wrong. If it's your choice, I respect that."

He shrugs. His face is red. "I haven't met the right woman, I guess. I'm pretty picky."

Despite my initial reaction, it's not so surprising. There's an innocent wildness about him. I look him over. His hair hasn't been cut in ages. Even in a humble T-shirt and jeans, his body is lean and beautiful.

"What are you thinking?" he whispers.

"I'm thinking that you're a poem," I say honestly.

He laughs and looks away, his cheeks turning a deeper scarlet. "No. Uh-uh. A poem is words. I'm flesh and blood."

"Are you?" I reach out to touch him again.

Slowly, I trace my finger down his arm, bare beneath his short sleeve. I follow the forked paths of the veins on his forearm.

His breathing is fast and shallow.

"Huh. How about that." My fingertips curl over his hand. "You really are flesh and blood."

His eyelids flicker, and his mouth opens.

"Kate!" Mikki hollers from the doorway. "Bus leaves in thirty seconds. Get your ass on it or we find a new singer in San Diego. Oh, hey, Benjamin Bunny," she chirps, giving me a sly smile.

"Shut it, Mik." I stub out my cigarette and push away from the wall. "I'll see you there," I say to Ben, who hasn't moved. He's trying so hard to keep his eyes on my face. But they keep drifting to the tattoos curling over my shoulders and the dip of cleavage above my black bra. "Drive safe."

He nods. Words have clearly deserted him.

*

In San Diego, Ben steps into his performer shoes and inhabits the room a little more. We kill it onstage. I'm constantly aware of his presence by the merch table, and I feel it through my whole body when he takes a step away to merge with the crowd.

The next day, before we can hit the road again, his car breaks down.

"We'll have it ready for you in a week," says the mechanic in a jolly voice, like this is good news. Ben has his head in his hands.

"Cheer up." Jules slings a sisterly arm around him. "You can ride with us. Right, ladies? Plenty of room on the bus. We'll make a special trip down here on the way back. You can pick up

105

your car good as new."

"You sure that's okay with you?" Ben looks up at her hopefully, then at me.

"Of course," Amanda fills in when I don't answer. "Right, Kate?"

I spread my hands. "Totally okay."

And that's how Ben joins us on the bus to San Francisco.

The next show is more intense. He's taking possession of the stage. Starting to interact with the audience. Smiling, getting into the give-and-take of throwing your feelings out to the room and having the audience's feelings thrown right back at you.

After the show, I join him behind the club in what's become our little ritual. We make halting conversation and I run my finger up and down his arm. His soft hair stands on end and a shudder runs through his lean, beautiful body.

This time, I don't smoke. If I kiss him, all I want him to taste is me.

Jules pokes her head out the door and rolls her eyes.

"Well, if it isn't the high school sweethearts. Whispering, giggling, passing notes…"

That night on the bus, I stare at his profile against the dark window. The wheels whir on the highway.

I shouldn't fuck him. I shouldn't *kiss* him. We're on tour together. I've seen how screwing around can mess with that dynamic. And he's a virgin.

I so want to be his first.

I lean over. "Wanna talk?" I whisper.

He nods too fast.

"Back there?" I point to the back of the bus, which is separated by a pair of leopard-print curtains that sway and flutter. He follows me back. In relative privacy, we sit down, our knees touching.

"What do you want to talk about?" he asks.

"Anything."

He looks down at his lap. "I'm not good with such open-ended options."

"Then how about we don't talk?" The butterflies are back, crazed and flapping. "We can just...sit here. Together."

Suddenly, he takes my hand. He's nervous; he wets his lips. He's so earnest and sweet. When I squeeze his hand, he slides his arms around me. I do the same. We hold each other tightly. I feel the beat of his heart against my chest.

"I've never kissed anyone," he confesses. His curls tickle my forehead.

"Never?"

He shrugs, that shy smile fleeting across his face. "I've never found anyone I wanted to connect to that much. Music's my love. People are distractions."

"Aren't they, though?" I lean in closer. "Or maybe...you're just..." He leans in too. "Scared."

"Scared?" He looks like he's about to laugh. Our lips are a breath apart.

"Scared to let go. If someone fills your head the way music does, you might..."

"Go on."

"Fly apart."

"Maybe I will," he whispers.

"But you might just fly."

The moment stretches out. His gorgeous lips part. His breath is warm. He bites his lower lip, letting it pull between his teeth.

"Do you want to fly, Ben?"

His green eyes dart. To the left, to the right, back to my face.

Goosebumps spatter my skin, and my nipples ache, tight and hard in my black lace halter.

I've never been so turned on.

"I don't know what to do." A flush rises up his cheekbones. A trickle of sweat slides down his forehead.

I lick my lips. "I know. If we kiss, you'll be so pure. Like tasting the breath of angels."

"I'm no angel."

Now my heart's beating fast. As if it's *my* first time. I lean even closer and give him the littlest, tiniest kiss on the cheek.

And he attacks me.

In the best possible way.

I'm too surprised to kiss him back at first. His mouth is absolutely everywhere. He sucks on my lips, licks my neck, shoves his tongue into my ear. When he grips my arms, running his hands up and down the skin, I swear every inked flower and thorn springs to life under his grasp.

My breath comes in short bursts. His excitement is catching, and I give it right back to him with my lips on his jaw, his mouth, his throat.

Under my tongue, his pulse throbs with a primal beat.

Ben is definitely flesh and blood.

The tussle of give and take is driving me mad. It reverberates through my body like the energy from a show. I thrust my hands into his curls like I've wanted to for days. He twines his fingers in my shaggy pink hair and pulls me into a hard kiss. There's a lot of tongue, a lot of slurping and inexperienced eagerness.

I want it all.

I don't want to teach him right now, to mold his moves so they're sensual and suave. I want all the raw untutored desire.

The haunting passion in his music, made hot and real.

We're wrestling on the seat in a tangle of arms and legs, until I'm brought up short by his hard cock pressing into my thigh.

He freezes.

Kissing his neck, I work my hand between our entwined bodies to cup the bulge. He's rock-hard, about to burst through his frayed jeans, and I stroke his erection lightly through the soft, worn denim.

His whole body shudders.

"Is this okay?" I squeeze his rigid shaft, enjoying the perfect shape of his cock. "Do you like it when I touch you here?"

A strangled groan leaves his lips.

"God." His voice is hoarse. "Kate..."

"The way you say my name, baby." I pull him down for another kiss.

He jerks as I caress his cock. His hand is still tight in my hair, and his lean, beautiful body is pressed against mine. We're half-sitting, half-lying down on the bench in the back of the bus.

A sudden bump in the road makes us jump.

I peek through the crack in the curtains. Jules is stretched across two seats, snoring softly. Amanda has her hood pulled over her head. Mikki curls up with her lucky stuffed dinosaur that she hauls along on every tour, peacefully asleep. Jett, who's driving, has music playing on low and is either oblivious to what's happening back here, or pretending to be.

I turn back to Ben, whose green eyes are luminous in the dark.

"Now where were we?"

I'm cut off when he pushes me down onto the seat. When I bounce from the force of his eagerness, he immediately lifts his hands.

"Was that too hard? I'll be more careful—"

I put my finger to his lips. "I'll tell you if it's too hard."

His smile is gorgeous. He traces the edge of my black lace halter top.

"Don't hold back," I plead.

He seizes my breasts, squeezing them like he's been starving for this all his life. I stifle a moan as he rips off my top, pushes my tits together, and buries his face in the soft curves. Sucking, leaving love bites. His beard is soft, but it scratches my tender skin.

He's an animal right now. But I say he's an angel too.

My nipples ache with pure need. My pussy throbs beneath my short skirt in time with the pulse in Ben's neck. I've got my thumb on that pulse and my hand on his head like I can contain the inferno that's blazed up between us.

I grasp the hem of his faded T-shirt.

"Let go, baby," I whisper. "Let me see you too."

He straightens, helping me strip off his shirt. I take the opportunity to undo my bra and toss it away.

He's lithe and beautiful, dappled with soft dark hair. As I explore his chest, teasing his nipples into hard little nubs, I know my mouth's hanging open. I've seen a lot of bodies, but I'm in awe.

His palms are warm and a little rough. He runs them over the tattoos on my shoulders and stares at the silver barbells piercing my nipples.

"You're the most stunning woman I've ever seen," he whispers.

I twist my fingers in his curls. "And you're a perfect song."

The girls would shit themselves laughing if they heard me say that. But they aren't listening. Only Ben.

"Not perfect," he whispers. "Not a song."

He keeps tracing my tattoos until he gets up the courage to return to my breasts. Cupping them in his warm hands, he rubs his thumbs over my tight, puckered nipples and explores the silver piercings.

His shifts between shy and raging are driving me crazy. When he pinches my nipples hard, I gasp.

He looks up, green eyes filled with concern. "Did that hurt?"

"In the best way, baby," I assure him. "Keep going."

My panties are fucking soaked. I want him — I *need* him. I urge him to straddle me on the seat, and as he fondles my tits, I tug at his zipper to open his jeans.

He jerks toward me. His hands tighten on my breasts in excitement, trapping the soft curves. His cock pokes through his boxers, greeting my palm eagerly.

Oh yeah…he's so big, so silky, so absolutely rock-hard. A drop of liquid oozes from the tip and I rub it all over his flared head.

Piercing green eyes lock on mine with an intoxicating brew of worship and need.

"Katie," he pants. For the first time in my life, I don't mind the nickname. Ben can moan it any time he likes. He makes it into a song — a poem.

Inexperienced as he is, he doesn't need any guidance to buck his hips forward. He slides his dick through my grasp in a rhythm we both understand.

"Oh God, ohhhhh God," he gasps raggedly. I tease his balls, heavy and full. They fit perfectly in my palm.

I'm yearning for his cum. I want to see him lost in the throes of passion.

"You're close, aren't you, honey?" I murmur. "I'm going to

suck you. I think you'll really like that."

His reply is cut off by his muffled grunt as I stroke the heavy cock that throbs so invitingly.

"What about you?" he tries. "I want— Kate, I need— I want to make you feel good—"

He really is close. And I want to have my cock and eat it too.

"If I suck you off…" I flick out my tongue, swirling it around and around his hot, spongy skin. "Can you get hard for me again?"

He gasps, his hands clenching on my breasts.

"I need you inside me, Ben. You have no idea."

He drops his face to mine and groans into my neck, trying to stifle himself.

"I need you to fuck me, baby. I want to be your first."

When his lips close on my neck, I squeeze his dick in response.

He doesn't realize how hard he's sucking on my tender flesh. He doesn't know my neck will be covered in hickeys by the time he's done.

"I want that too, Kate." He grips my shoulders. His tongue is everywhere — my neck, my throat, my ear, in the hollow between my collarbones.

"Tell me."

"I want —" He swallows. "I want to cum in your mouth," he whispers. "I want to touch you and drink you in and make you feel amazing. I want you to be my first."

"Get naked, baby. Come up here and let me suck on you."

Feverishly, he unlaces his Chucks, peels off his socks and jeans and boxers. His beautiful cock springs free and he kneels above me, grabbing the back of the seat as the bus bumps along.

Oh, yes. This is what I've been wanting since I first saw Ben onstage. I want him in my mouth, I want his fucking essence inside me.

Lavishing attention on his silky head, I urge him to sink his cock deep in my mouth as I fondle his balls.

He's trying to make the pleasure last, but I'm not letting him. Not this time. Not when I want to taste his cum so badly. His hands clutch my hair, making tears spring to my eyes. His body takes over as he fucks my face, losing himself to the ecstasy of my lips and tongue all over his rigid dick.

He goes tense. He's trying not to cry out on this dark bus filled with sleeping people. He climaxes fast and hard, streams of cum splashing over my tongue.

I swallow and wipe my mouth with the back of my hand. Before I can say a word, he dives between my legs, pulling at my miniskirt. It comes off along with my panties, and I'm naked before him.

He spreads my legs and takes a minute to stare. Then he gently traces my labia, opening them so he can see every bit of me. I bite my lip as big fingers stroke my wet, wet pussy.

"Oh my God," he whispers. I know he's found the sparkling barbell piercing my clit hood. "Can I...touch it?"

He looks up at me, pleading. Sweet Jesus, he's shaking with excitement.

"I'd be mad if you didn't," I tease.

He caresses my swollen clit, rubbing the exposed tip until my thighs shake. Then he takes a deep breath and presses his beautiful face to my cunt.

His mouth's everywhere again. Broad, flat licks, like he's trying to press his whole tongue against every crevice of my pussy. He's so enthusiastic, so fucking eager.

"Whoa, stallion," I gasp, fisting his curls. "Slow down."

"God, I'm sorry. Did I hurt you?" Even in the dark, his cheeks flame scarlet. I feel the heat rolling off his body.

"It's not a race, baby. We've got time. I just want to feel you."

Taking a deep breath, he dives in again, lapping my clit. He flicks the ring with his tongue, and I bite my fist to keep back a moan. He explores my soft flesh slowly now, lavishing licks all over my cunt. I'm so sensitive and open to him and so fucking wet.

Taking his hand, I guide him to my tight hole. I moan when he probes me with two fingers, massaging and exploring.

I struggle to keep my voice down. "Ben, I'm going to — oh, don't stop — keep doing that —"

He sucks on my clit. He's shuddering with excitement between my sprawled thighs. I have no doubt that his cock is hard again, poking into the seat of the bus.

But he's careful now. Pushing down the stallion, keeping it bay, while with infinite patience he flicks the little nub at the apex of my cunt.

My thighs shake uncontrollably. I can't remember being so in tune with another person. An instrument played with such total attention.

His fingers twist inside my cunt. His tongue ceaselessly licks my hypersensitive clit. And all the sensations are spilling into overload, because it's too much, I can't take how good it is, we're the centers of each other's worlds right now and it's more than I can bear.

I come.

Hard.

My pussy closes on his fingers in a long spasm. Squeezing him, carrying us both away. His breath hitches, and I know he's startled by the sensation of being so powerfully gripped. But he's so sweet; he doesn't stop licking until my thighs go slack and I stroke his curls.

"Ben," I sigh.

He climbs on top to kiss me. I savor my tart juices smeared over those beautiful lips. I suck on his tongue, wanting every last drop of my flavor mixed with his breath, until he groans and pushes his hot erection between my legs.

He's big. He's young. He's innocent and wildly excited. And I can't wait another second.

Grasping his cock, I rub him up and down my slick valley, soaking him in the juices that well up. Finally, I let him slide until he lodges at the opening to my pussy.

"Right there, baby." I wrap my arms around his trembling body, wanting to hold him close at the moment that he loses it. "Go ahead. Come inside."

He pushes slowly, so fucking slowly, sweat dripping off his forehead onto mine, as the flared head of his cock opens me a little at a time. I bite my lip at his size.

"Are you sure?" he whispers. He's barely inside me, and he's afraid to push. "You feel so — so —"

I kiss his cheeks, his eyelids, his lips. His broad cock, rubbing against my sensitive opening, is driving me insane.

"Take me, Ben." I lift my hips.

There's a sudden big thrust that makes me gasp. But I hold him tight, murmuring sweet words as he sinks in deep, stretching and filling me. I tell him how wonderful he is as he begins to move.

In his excitement, he's gentle and rough all at once. His green eyes are wide as he plunges his cock into me again and again. Like when he sucked on my neck, he doesn't realize how hard he's fucking me. The breath flies from me as he grinds against my clit. As he unleashes all his eager unrestrained force.

It actually does hurt a little. He's big, and his movements are jerky. But the pain is a pinch of cayenne pepper in a froth of hot, melted chocolate. It adds the perfect kick of heat, an edge that I love.

I run my hands over his lean back and beautiful ass, encouraging him.

"You're so beautiful, Ben. I love the way you feel inside me. I love being close to you like this."

He shudders, his cock pulsing inside me. He's going so deep, fucking me into a frenzy. As I lean into the pain edging the pleasure, embracing it, I open to him further and further. I'm getting more excited, close to orgasm again.

"Ben, I'm gonna...oh God." I rub my clit frantically.

"You're touching yourself. Fuck," he breathes.

The unexpected curse makes my pussy tighten. He must notice, because he does it again.

"Do it," he pants, driving the point home with hard, heavy thrusts. "Rub your clit while I fuck you. Come on my cock, Katie, come so hard for me."

I clench up tight. Then I melt. I quiver, spasming all over Ben. On his rock-hard flesh, buried deep in my pussy. It's sudden and intimate and I have the strange feeling that I know him very well.

He whispers "Katie, Katie, Katie," as I come. Undoing me even more, until I'm a puddle beneath him and he stares into my eyes, his face twisting in the throes of his climax. His thrusts are even deeper, more intense, as he releases a flood of cum inside me.

Finally, he slips from my pussy. We hold each other close, sweaty and content. His heart is racing, and I relish each beat as it slows.

"Still think I'm an angel?" he whispers.

"I think you're Ben," I whisper back. "You're a sexy beast, but there's some angel in there too."

He grins shyly. "I fantasized about cumming on you," he whispers in my ear, stretching his body over mine. "That first show, the night you took your shirt off. I thought about you throwing me the rest of your clothes. Once you were naked, I came all over your gorgeous breasts and belly and even your pussy. And since you couldn't perform like that, I cleaned you off with a T-shirt from the merch table. Made sure I didn't miss a spot." He rubs his nose sweetly along my jaw. "You came too while I was doing that. Really hard."

I smile into his shoulder. "Well, there goes my theory of you being a beautiful innocent."

"Which part? Beautiful or innocent?"

I smack his ass lightly. "Ooh, sassy."

He chuckles, but soon he stiffens in my arms.

"What is it, baby?"

"Katie, I don't want this to be a one-night stand. If it is for you —" He takes a deep breath. "Tell me. Don't spare my feelings. I'm just being honest."

Jesus. He's young, he's unworldly, and everything is a first for him.

But I don't want it to be a one-night stand either.

I want to wake up in bed next to Ben on a lazy Sunday morning and hear him call me Katie while we fix breakfast. I want us to pick up our guitars and make dirty, sweet, crazy music together. I want to fuck him until we're completely fucked out.

I want to be with him.

"You really want to try to be together?" I ask.

He nods.

"Are you sure? I can be loud…obnoxious…"

"You're incredible, is what you are."

I kiss his sweaty neck. "And you're an angel."

He grins. For the first time, I see a glint of dry humor. "Okay, Katie. The angel thing? *That's* obnoxious."

I give him a last cuddle before we pull on our clothes. "Sorry, baby. You're just a walking piece of heaven on earth."

This time, I'm the one who gets my ass swatted. It bodes well for the future. We tiptoe out from behind the leopard-print curtains like triumphant teenagers, and I fall asleep with a smile.

In the morning, over breakfast in a diner with the band, I can't help but open my mouth.

"You guys were passed out last night." I help myself to more maple syrup, stealing a veggie sausage link from Amanda's plate. "And I mean *passed out.* You must have been steamrolled by that last show."

Jules sips her coffee, looking at me demurely over the rim, and flutters her sparkly, fake blue lashes. "Oh, you mean, the way we slept through you taking Ben's virginity?"

I choke on the veggie sausage, while Mikki lets out a whoop and a drumroll on the table. Quickly, I glance at Ben, who's crammed into the booth on my other side. I'm more worried about his embarrassment than mine.

His cheeks flush, but he shrugs and grins. He doesn't look traumatized. Far from it.

In fact, he takes my hand under the table. I can't remember the last time I let someone do that.

"We tried to be quiet, ladies. Not my fault you value eavesdropping more than your beauty sleep."

"God, Kate," Amanda says, "Stop smiling like that. You look like a—"

"A fucking marshmallow," Jules supplies.

"She is." Ben squeezes my hand. "She's the biggest marshmallow in the world."

"Shut up, all of you." I resume eating my pancakes with dignity.

"Okay, *Katie*," Mikki sings, and the girls dissolve in giggles.

I'm too happy to give a shit. Ben leans over to kiss me, licking a drop of maple syrup from my lip. I don't care what he says; I've tasted the breath of an angel, and there's no going back.

THE WEDDING AND THE WOLF
A *Priceless* Story

Part I: The Wedding
Christina

"What are you thinking about?"

My fiancé leaned across the café table to tuck my hair behind my ear. The summer wind stirred my long heavy waves.

I looked up innocently from the remains of our dinner.

"Oh, nothing."

"You're gonna make me guess?"

He twisted a lock of hair around his finger. I eyed his big hand, so close to my face. When he pulled, I shivered pleasantly. Wondering, with just a touch of nerves, whether anyone was watching.

"Come on, Patrick." I crossed my legs. "We both know you're a mind-reader. Tell me. What am I thinking?"

He laughed. That was one of the things I loved about Patrick: how easily he laughed these days.

When we'd met in college, he'd been a cold bastard. Damaged, trying to patch himself together, an island who thought he needed no one.

Now he was my future husband, grinning at me from across

the table. The evening sunlight glinted off his short, light brown hair. His pale blue eyes were soft, his broad shoulders relaxed.

But under that brawny teddy-bear exterior, there lurked a wolf.

Hungry, savage, dominating.

And I wouldn't have it any other way.

"Okay, babe." He tugged on my hair. "You're thinking that it's Friday night and you're going to forget about work until Monday."

I wrinkled my nose at him. "I don't need to think about that. You're the one who takes your work home with you. All finance and figures and obsession. I don't dream about, like, *marketing solutions.*"

"Fine. You're thinking you're going to take the last cookie." He nodded toward the plate of amaretti on the table.

Snagging the lone cookie, I took a bite and beamed at him. "That's already a given."

"You're thinking that you're my princess, but you're on your way to earning a spanking tonight."

That got us a glare from the next table. My cheeks flushed. "Getting warmer, Patrick."

"Am I?" His hand found my knee and slid up my thigh. I snapped my legs together, trapping his hand between them. "Mmm, yeah. I think I am."

I laughed, suddenly breathless. "Dirty boy." I held out the half-eaten cookie. He gobbled it and nipped at my fingers.

"Hmmm. You're thinking that the next time your mom calls to 'discuss' the wedding, you're going to let me carry you off and make you an honest woman…" He smirked at me. "… Without the benefit of a hundred and fifty people watching."

"Honestly? I'm about this close to letting you do that." I held my fingers an inch apart. "But no. The next time she calls, I'll just put you on the phone. She *loves* you. She's the only person you even try to charm."

He squeezed my leg. "Watch it, girl."

"I'm thinking…" I leaned across the table. "…About our wedding night."

His brows lifted. With his free hand, the one that wasn't trapped between my legs, he laced his fingers through mine.

"It'll be our first time," I whispered. "As a married couple. It's a big deal."

"Oh?" His mouth quirked in a half-grin. "You want me to carry you across the threshold? Worship you with rose petals? Pop a cork on the champagne?"

I toyed with my wine glass, watching him. "I wouldn't drink alone on our wedding night."

And Patrick wouldn't drink at all. He hadn't touched alcohol in years.

His face turned serious. "You want all that, don't you, love? I want you to be happy."

My breath caught. Grand gestures were not Patrick's love language.

"Yeah, I guess I do. But I also want you to be yourself. I want us to be Patrick and Christina." I leaned forward, my voice dropping to a whisper. "And I want the wolf."

"Are you sure?"

Something in his deep voice made me shiver.

"Yes."

"On your wedding night?"

I nodded, excitement suddenly heating my body, welling between my legs.

"You want a lot, Christina." His voice took on the cool tones that promised pulling back the curtain on dark delights. "I always knew you were a greedy girl."

"I want champagne and rose petals, but I also want you to be mean." I bit my lip, widening my eyes. Would Patrick say no? "I want you to have your way with me."

"You should be careful what you wish for."

Squirming on the cafe chair, I squeezed my thighs together. Patrick's hand still pressed between them. Rubbing the soft flesh, pinching it. My pussy ached, and my stomach was doing flip-flops.

"Get up, girl." The quiet command got me instantly to my feet. "We're going home. Let's find out if this is really what you want."

*

Twenty minutes later, I knelt on the bedroom floor in our apartment. I couldn't look away from the hard ridge in Patrick's slacks as he slowly, deliberately unbuckled his belt. Metal sounded on metal with a clink of finality.

The lights were out, and a rim of red sunset gleamed through the open window

Under my short skirt, my pussy pulsed in anticipation. My bare knees wriggled against the soft carpet. We'd chosen a rug with a thick, cushy pile for exactly this reason. So I could kneel for him, crawl to him, without the added bite of a hard floor.

When I reached for his zipper, he gripped my wrist. "Not 'til I say so."

You could say his reaction was predictable, but even now, I didn't always know what to expect with Patrick. He kept me off-balance in the bedroom. He loved to toy with me, playing games and wreaking havoc with my response.

But we hadn't done it in awhile. Between the stress of planning our wedding, the pressures of dealing with our families, and the responsibilities of work, our lovemaking — when it happened — had been gentle and sweet. Tender.

All teddy bear, no wolf.

Now, his voice was cold. Merciless. ""I've gone easy on you for awhile, Christina. All soft and sweet, being so careful." Dammit, he really was a mind reader. His grip tightened on my wrist. "I'm not going easy on you anymore."

An involuntary moan dropped from my lips.

"Take your shirt off." The words were quiet, but knife-edged. "Look at me while you do it."

Gazing up at him, I pulled my sleeveless silk blouse over my head. Cool blue eyes roved over my sweaty skin.

"And the bra."

Quickly, I undid my lacy bra, knowing better than to look away. Our bedroom was warm, but I shivered.

Patrick's eyes stroked me like ice. My nipples hardened into aching points.

He knew exactly how hard it was for me to sit still. How impatient I got. Squirming under his stare, I reached for his fly again.

"Hands behind your back, girl," he ordered.

I obeyed, my eyes glued to the bulge in Patrick's slacks. Like me, he was dressed up for his work day. Patrick always dressed carefully.

His zipper came down with a scrape. My mouth watered as he freed his cock from his boxers.

Heat curled through me at the sight of the big, carved shaft so close to my lips. I squeezed my hands into fists behind my back, clenching my thighs together. My pussy was damp just from the clean scent of his slacks, the musk of his cock and heavy balls, the smell of his leather belt, all within licking distance.

I couldn't wait any longer.

Impulsively, I took him in my hands. His cock was hot and hard and satiny smooth. Diving face-first into his crotch, I sucked eagerly.

A sharp inhale was my reward. Involuntarily, he pushed into my mouth with a groan. His precum tasted so good, and if I sucked fast enough, maybe he'd come in my mouth...

A firm grip on my hair forced my chin up.

"You disobeyed me, Christina. I'm not happy."

Liar. His dick was rigid in my mouth, and a flush stained his pale cheeks. It took a lot to get Patrick to flush.

I sucked harder, wanting his pleasure and my punishment all at the same time. My head spun with excitement.

He moved back abruptly, pulling his cock from my lips. Scooping me up, he threw me on the bed.

"Arms above your head." His voice was as cold as a winter wind.

Dizzy with need, I obeyed. Swiftly, Patrick lashed my wrists to the headboard with the rope he kept in his nightstand. I arched toward him, half-naked and aroused.

Huge hands snaked down my body, deliberately fondling my breasts. Every movement said *mine*. When he rubbed his thumbs over my nipples in slow circles, smiling coldly as they puckered even tighter, I moaned. Loudly.

"Slut," he said softly. "As if I had any doubt. You can't even wait for my cock."

"Please, please don't make me." I arched toward him. When

I first met Patrick, I'd been embarrassed to beg. I wanted to, but each request was a wrestling match with my pride.

Now, I had zero problems with it. I babbled as he unceremoniously lifted my ass to unzip my skirt, pulling it over my hips. When he peeled off my silky panties, slick with my juices, he held them to his face and inhaled deeply.

That got me. He'd never done that before.

A whimper left my mouth.

"What's wrong, babe?" His voice was soft, mocking. "Don't tell me you're embarrassed. I've smelled your girl juice countless times. You can't hide how fucking wet I get you."

I gasped when he crouched over me, one big hand squeezing my breast and my panties in his fist. He brushed the glossy crotch over my lips.

"Jerk," I whispered.

I felt so naked, bound and sweating beneath him. Patrick loomed over me, broad and rugged, his chest and shoulders pale as marble even in the heat. His belt still dangled, unbuckled, the edges brushing my hips.

He wrapped the soaked crotch of my panties around two big fingers and pushed them into my mouth.

A haze descended over my vision as I fell into the moment. Yielding to my fiancé, sucking frantically on the tangy fabric, licking his fingers.

Satisfied with my response, he pulled his hand away and tossed my panties on the floor. His belt slid from its loops with a menacing rustle.

Without warning, he pushed my thighs apart and traced the edge of the metal buckle over my soaked lips.

"God," I whispered.

"Two years together, babe." His icy eyes roved over my

126

pleading face, my arching breasts, my spread pussy. The buckle, cool and hard and smooth, outlined my most secret flesh, hot and melting for him. "Two and a half, really." One finger pushed back the hood of my clit, and the tip of the buckle circled the exposed nub. "And you're still an impatient little brat who can't even wait two minutes for what she wants. You're greedy, Christina. You're desperate for my cock."

"Please..."

"You want me to be mean, babe?" He toyed with my helpless pussy, opening my soaked flesh with his fingers and running the buckle around my entrance. "You want the wolf to come for you on your wedding night?"

"Yes, yes, yes," I panted.

"Then no sex between now and the wedding. Of any kind."

"What?" My head bounced up from the pillows.

"You heard me, Christina. You don't touch yourself, you don't come. If I catch you breaking that rule, you'll be severely punished, and not in a way you'll like."

I stared up at him, breathing shallowly. I could imagine what Patrick would do. Give me the silent treatment, ignore me — all the things I'd hate the most.

It was a game, of course. I could use my safe word any time. But I preferred to play. Just as I was once too proud to beg, now I was too proud to whip out the safe word unless I truly wanted the action to grind to a halt.

"You're joking."

He leaned down, his breath caressing my neck. "Babe, it's two weeks away. Don't tell me you can't hold out that long. You're that hungry? That needy? That horny?"

I strained toward him. "What about you?"

"I'll follow the same rules." His cool voice washed over me.

"I don't have any problem waiting for you. *You're* the impatient little slut in this house."

I moaned, sweat beading on my chest.

"What do you say, princess?" He pinched both my nipples at once. I rose off the bed toward him. "Are you going to follow my orders? Do you want to earn your wedding night?"

"Yes, Patrick," I panted.

"That's my good girl."

"What about right now?" I swung my legs up to hook my ankles on his broad shoulders. My cheerleading days had ended when I graduated college, but I was still flexible. Strong. Patrick tried to cover his reaction, but I could read him as well as he read me.

"Look at me. I'm all —" I lifted my ass toward him, shamelessly displaying my arousal. "And you're all —" I stared at the unyielding bulge in his slacks. "Excited."

As frosty as his eyes were, the chill evaporated into hot lust. Scalding my body, stoking my need. He swallowed. I lived for the moments when Patrick lost his composure. When his control cracked.

"All you need to do is unzip your pants, baby," I coaxed. "You can be fucking me in two seconds. Do you really want to stop now?"

The muscles flexed in his shoulders as he crouched over me. I felt so exposed suddenly, bound by the rope, caged by his arms and legs. Patrick always felt huge on top of me — inside me. But it wasn't just his size that made me shiver and shake. He had a way of fucking me at times, hard and careless, that made me feel little.

Little, and shatteringly aroused.

Patrick gave me a long look. He got off the bed, walked to

the head, and took my hair in a tight grip.

I tried to jerk my head up, but he pressed it against the pillow. The pressure only got me more excited — my belly clenching, my pussy fluttering.

When he twisted his hand in my hair, I winced.

"Maybe I should leave you here for a while, Christina. There are dishes to do...bills to pay...you can think about how to behave for me while I take care of our household."

Dammit.

What had I started by summoning the wolf?

"Please untie me," I said in a small voice. A breathy voice, the voice that came out only with Patrick. "I'll behave. You don't have to do all the dishes."

His face softened a fraction. He unknotted the rope around my wrists. "Go take a cold shower. I'll see you afterwards."

"You first." I looked pointedly at his bulging crotch. "You look like you need it."

I was hoping for a smack on the ass, or at least a smile, but Patrick was having none of it.

"Go," he said. "Cool off. And don't even think about touching your little pussy. I'll know if you do."

The order only made me hotter. Just the experience of being commanded by Patrick did me in. I considered putting up a fuss, for fun, but Patrick's cool blue gaze made me think better of it.

I stalked off to the bathroom. When I emerged, the kitchen was clean and all the dishes were done.

I found Patrick in our room. He'd changed into a T-shirt and boxers and was sketching in bed.

"What are you drawing?" I leaned over him, kissing the top of his head. My long wet hair dangled in his face, and my breast

129

brushed his cheek.

"Us," he said without looking up. "Put some clothes on."

I snorted and pulled a short nightie and some fresh panties from our dresser. Climbing into bed beside him, I snuggled up. "Chaste enough for you?"

He laughed and put his arm around me.

"Sure. You like it?" He showed me his sketchpad.

Normally, Patrick drew from life. Me, architecture, models in art class. Our bedroom walls were covered with his framed drawings. He loved to draw me after we had sex; a dozen versions of a thoroughly-fucked Christina gazed down at us from the walls.

But recently, he'd started drawing from his imagination. I stared at the fantastical image taking shape on the page: a half-naked, dark-haired bride.

Her ethereal veil and elegant bouquet made a sharp contrast to her bared breasts and arched back. Her pure white gown, unbuttoned and bunched around her hips, fell in folds to the ground. She was caught about the waist by a huge, shadowy figure that could be a man or a beast.

His fingers in her mouth. His hand ruining her gorgeous hairdo. Her expression of ecstasy.

I swallowed. Patrick knew how to get under my skin, but more than that, this was what lived under his skin. Together, we visited our dark places. Every so often, he needed to release the beast.

"You're a very talented artist," I said airily. "I don't see why you need to pursue a career in finance. Quit your day job already."

He kissed my forehead. "You want to be the breadwinner, babe? Support us both?"

I curled up in his embrace. "It would be poetic justice, don't you think?"

He grinned.

These days, we rarely talked about how we met — how our sexual relationship began. It wasn't a skeleton in the closet; it just didn't feel relevant anymore. We'd been a couple much longer than I'd been Patrick's companion.

But at the beginning, we'd had an arrangement, and it involved him paying me for kinky sex.

Our black cat, Ember, slipped through the crack in the door and jumped on the bed, making herself comfortable at my side.

"Hey, girl." I petted her as Patrick put the pad aside.

When he cuddled me close, I draped my leg over him and hugged his bulky thigh between mine.

"No tempting me after tonight," he ordered, tempering the command with a kiss on the forehead.

I laughed, drawing a line down his chest with my fingertip. "Baby, I don't have to do anything to tempt you. I tempt you just by walking around. I tempt you by existing."

He rubbed his nose against mine. "Someone's gotten a big head these last two years."

"Your fault."

We lay snuggled together as the curtains fluttered in the breeze. Patrick had his quirks, and one of them was always keeping a window open a crack.

He had a dislike of feeling caged. He wanted to breathe.

The fact that he'd asked me to spend my life with him had more significance than most people realized. Back at the beginning, in college, we'd been too gun-shy to pursue anything more than an arrangement — for months. He believed relationships were not to be trusted, and I thought I had to put on a show to be loved.

I kissed Patrick's chest. He made a happy sighing noise, pulling me closer. Those days seemed very far away now. But I didn't take it for granted, for one single second, that he believed in us enough to put his trust in me for a lifetime.

*

The next two weeks were the busiest, and the fastest, of my life.

Mostly, it was a good kind of busy. But as the wedding approached, anticipation mounted, and little incidents picked away at my joy. Tiny needles, no big deal on their own, but irritating once they added up.

My mom insisted that we change the seating so Patrick's parents weren't at the same table, but Patrick's mom, Lee Anna, had called me a week earlier to request the opposite.

"I want us all to sit together—me, Patrick's dad, Nick and Eddie, and my second husband. We've been married almost six years, I want him and Patrick's dad to finally meet. Oh, this is going to be a beautiful occasion...a big adventure...one loving family..."

She sounded misty, and I wondered if she was day drinking.

Our photographer got sick. Our caterer double-booked.

Dexter, my ex, had the nerve to send a fake, sugary card. Jess, Patrick's ex, sent one too, but I put hers on the mantel instead of the garbage can. I liked Jess. But a day later, I caught Patrick eyeing the card, his huge shoulders hunched. Maybe it reminded him of all the years he spent in hiding, ashamed of his desires.

Posing as a teddy bear, stifling the wolf.

I put the card away in a drawer.

The little incidents piled up.

And as excited as I was to be getting married to Patrick, I was getting incredibly frustrated at his ban on sex.

I'd agreed, of course. I wanted the wolf.

But I could use a fucking release from all the stress.

The rehearsal dinner was beautiful. Near the end of the night, though, it began to unravel.

"Christina, you have to change the seating,"my mom hissed, eyeing Patrick's family across the room. Lee Anna and Patrick's dad, Dennis, had started the evening getting along, but were obviously no longer on speaking terms. Meanwhile, his brother Nick was busy getting drunk and loud while my college-aged cousins enthusiastically joined him. His youngest brother, Eddie, looked completely overwhelmed by all the noise and people.

I tried to hold it together. "Mom, since when are you so afraid of a little family drama? It wouldn't be a Ramirez gathering without it. Don't be scared just 'cause it's coming from my in-laws this time."

"Scared? Who's scared? Are *you* scared? Don't tell me you're having second thoughts, Christina. Patrick's a real catch. You won't do any better than him."

I didn't tell her she'd said the same thing about Dexter. Instead, I grabbed an empty glass and filled it. "Mom, have some wine."

The next afternoon, kneeling beside Patrick in front of the priest, the snowy folds of my gown spread out around me, I tried to focus on what mattered.

My love. Our life together. What we shared.

I peeked over at him from under my veil. Patrick looked serene. Peaceful. Huge in his tux. He would've been satisfied having three people at our wedding: him, me, and a justice of the peace. But he knew I wanted a big church wedding, a party afterward.

He wanted me to be happy.

When he caught me looking, a smile tugged at his mouth.

My mind jumped ahead to later. To tonight. I took a deep breath and focused on the ceremony so I wouldn't notice all the suddenly phallic-looking candles, or the fact that I was kneeling beside my love.

Afternoon merged into evening just as we made our grand entrance at the reception hall overlooking a lake. We danced, we ate. Candles glittered everywhere, and the huge windows showed a magnificent sunset on the lake.

Patrick didn't let go of my hand, and I didn't want him to. Everything was going without a hitch.

At least it seemed that way. Until I noticed at dinner that Patrick's family — who did end up sitting together — was arguing, and my aunts weren't speaking to my sister Alexis, and half my friends from college were nowhere to be seen.

"You okay, babe?" Patrick ran his thumb over my lips.

I fought the urge to tell him not to ruin my makeup. What was wrong with me? I wanted his touch. I was dying for him to fuck me.

"I'm fine!" I chirped.

"Liar," he said calmly, but his blue eyes were worried.

"Really. Whatever issues people have, they're not my problem right now. We're married and I'm going to enjoy it."

"Damn right." He grinned and kissed me.

Outside the ladies room, I was waylaid by my mom.

"Christina, you're going to fix your lipstick? Good. What is going on with your friends from college? That Marcus, I swear he's high. His eyes were bloodshot when I talked to him. And his girlfriend, Amelia? Why does she have to have that expression all the time?"

"Mom, that's what she looks like."

Out of the corner of my eye, my sister Alexis was heading straight for me in her champagne-colored matron of honor dress.

I grabbed her hand before Mom could snatch her away. "I need some air. "

Outside behind the wedding hall, as the velvet sky twinkled with stars, an unmistakable scent wafted toward us. Under a tree, we found Marcus and Amelia passing around a fucking joint with Patrick's brother Nick, my cousin Gabrio, and... Patrick's mom.

I marched up in my wedding gown, snatched the joint from Marcus, and took a drag. Everyone cheered.

"Christina!" Alexis groaned. "It's going to smell up your dress."

"It's her wedding, woman," Marcus said amiably. "Lady Christina, take as much as you want."

"Awwww, such a beautiful bride." Lee Anna smiled at me, her eyes glazed.

Nick grinned. Behind him, Eddie lay peacefully in the grass. "Where's your happy husband?" His eyes flicked over my shoulder. "Oh, hey, bro."

A hand descended on my shoulder — Patrick's. Staring at the scene, he palmed his forehead.

"Jesus Christ, Mom."

Everyone burst into laughter, and even I began to giggle as the weed started to kick in. But Patrick noticeably tensed, and when no one else was looking, I saw him shoot me an icy look.

Sudden panic arose in my chest. *Oh shit. Oh shit oh shit oh shit.*

Then his palm engulfed mine. His blue eyes warmed, and a menacing grin tugged at his mouth.

He leaned down towards my ear.

"Soon," he whispered.

Now it was my turn to tense. Everywhere, from the goosebumps on my neck to the flexing of my calves. My belly clenched. I wanted what Patrick had to give, but I was so far from that headspace right now.

Would I be able to let go?

Would I be able to handle the wolf?

Somehow, Patrick and I got back inside. We cut the wedding cake, we fed each other the sweet crumbs and sugary frosting. We danced, we talked and laughed with our guests. If anyone was still fighting, they seemed to have put their arguments aside for now.

We left for the hotel amidst yells and cheers. Alexis cupped her hands to her mouth and called "Make some good loving!"

Part II: The Wolf

Patrick

When we arrived at our hotel room, I swept Christina up into my arms, unlocked the door, and carried her inside. She laughed, clinging to my neck. She was a sweet armful, but I could barely feel her through all the layers of satin.

The room had everything Christina asked for: champagne chilling in a bucket of ice, a big bouquet of red roses on the dresser.

She smiled up at me. She was still impeccably made up, her hair falling in loose curls over her bare shoulders. I got an image of ruining her gorgeous hairdo, smearing her makeup, ripping her sparkling dress from her body.

"We're really married," she whispered.

"Mm-hm." I gently squeezed the back of her neck.

I'd been leery of marriage for a long time. Of the ritualized commitment. My parents' marriage had imploded, and I'd spent years dealing with the fallout. But the longer Christina and I were together, the more inescapable the truth became: we wanted to spend our lives together.

She wanted all of me, the dark and the light. I felt the same way about her.

And though she'd been a good girl these past two weeks,

never breaking my rule of chastity, there were times I'd regretted it. We both could have used a good fucking.

I set her down on the thick hotel carpet and she wrapped her arms around me. I hugged her gently, mindful of the wedding dress between us.

The roughness would come soon enough.

"My wife," I whispered, grinning like a fool.

Christina's smile beamed out, lighting up her face. "My husband." She cupped my cheeks in her hands.

I tipped her chin up and gave her a soft kiss on the lips. "Do you need anything?"

"Just you."

I released her. "Put your veil back on, Christina." Her arched brows rounded in a question she didn't ask. Obediently, she went to pin it in place.

As soon as her back was turned, I flicked out the lights.

Her gasp curled through my body. A match from my pocket flared, illuminating the shadows. In seconds, a single candle was lit on the dresser, another in the bathroom. But the room was still dark, the air thick with anticipation.

"I see you, little lamb," I said softly.

There was a rustle. Christina was moving, hurrying into the bathroom. She halted in front of the mirror, the door open, her back to me.

I grabbed the ice-filled bucket of champagne and followed.

Candlelight outlined her gauzy veil and the elegant fall of her gown, the long dark hair tumbling down her back. A gasp left her mouth when I grasped her bare shoulders.

"What do we have here?" I pressed my mouth against her veil. "A beautiful bride."

She tried to turn to me, but I held her in place, bunching the fragile veil in my hand. "Are you scared, little lamb? You asked for the wolf on your wedding night."

She gave me a look from under her thick dark lashes. "Yes, but—"

Deliberately, I stroked her neck, relishing the eager throbbing of her pulse. When I bit that same spot, she gasped. "Just what I was hungry for tonight. A sweet little girl."

"Please don't hurt me." Her plea was breathy and excited, low and warm. Her skin flushed under my hand.

Pulling her close, I curled my fingers around her throat. "Don't worry, little lamb. I won't hurt you...much." She shuddered in my embrace. "I'll just ruin you for your husband, sweet one."

"But I'm yours." She ran shaky hands over mine, struggling for control. It really had been too long since we played this way. "I am your bride."

I chuckled. "You are now. And I'm going to keep you."

Spinning her around, I seized her mouth in a kiss. My hand sank into her carefully styled hair. Her fists closed on my tuxedo jacket, pulling at it. Her mouth was eager and alive as she yielded, opening to my tongue, her breath quickening as she kissed me back.

I ran my hands peremptorily over her cheeks, her neck, her bare shoulders and exposed cleavage. "You're so hot. So flushed. Let's cool you off."

Turning her to face the mirror, I reached for the bucket of ice. Christina clutched the bathroom counter, her coal-dark eyes glazed as she stared at our reflection.

The pure, beautiful bride, lipstick kissed off and full lips swollen.

And the beast, looming behind her in a tuxedo.

"What are you going to do?" Her voice wavered.

"You'll see."

I grasped her hair and ran an ice chip over her exposed throat. It melted instantly. Rivulets ran down her warm skin.

"You'll get my dress wet." She was flushed, panting with excitement.

"Mm-hm." I pushed another ice cube between the tight, embroidered top of her gown and her bare back.

"Patrick!" She grabbed my wrists. I twisted free and covered her mouth with one hand. Christina moaned, licking my palm. Her tongue was hot and eager as she wriggled in my grasp.

"Patrick isn't here, sweet. You're at the mercy of the wolf now. Understand?"

She nodded frantically. Releasing her, I took two handfuls of ice, the cold biting my palms, and rubbed them over the soft curves of her tits. Water dripped onto the exquisite fabric. She cried out, bucking against me.

"Look at you, little lamb. So excited, and we've barely gotten started."

"Please," she gasped.

"Poor baby. There must be somewhere else that's even hotter, isn't there? Somewhere that really needs cooling off. Lift up your pretty dress for me."

Christina's back arched, pressing her ass into my thigh. Arousal flared in her eyes. In that breathy little voice I knew so well, she whispered, "You do it. Please. I'm embarrassed..."

I laughed. "Oh no, sweet. I know exactly what you are under all that beautiful, virginal white. You're a slut. You're dying to be fucked senseless by the wolf. And you're going to lift up your dress and show me your wet little panties, because I say so. You're going to give me every inch of your body. You're going to

140

do whatever I say."

Shaking with excitement, she gripped the layers of gleaming white material and lifted them to her waist. I ran my fingers over her smooth legs, the frilly garter she'd kept on above one knee, savoring the goosebumps on her thighs.

"Hmmm, what's this?" Sliding a hand between her legs, I found the dampness on her silky white panties. More than dampness — she was fucking soaked. Pressing in, I rubbed her swollen clit through the fabric.

The panties were barely an excuse for covering her pussy — just a little triangle of snowy lace containing her neatly trimmed dark hair. The fabric narrowed between her legs...into a thong.

What the fuck? Christina never wore thongs. She couldn't stand them.

I pinched her bare ass. When she cried out, I squeezed her mound hard.

"You're enjoying this, little lamb. Aren't you? You like being felt up in your wedding dress."

"Oh God..."

Holding her tightly to me, I rubbed my raging cock against her ass, pushing against the confines of my tux.

"That's right. There's my pussy." I pulled the delicate lace away from her crotch to fit my hand inside. Those panties would tear with one yank. Spreading her soaked lips, drawing out the moment, I smiled coldly at our reflections in the mirror. "All mine. Too bad for your husband. Don't cover it like this again."

Without warning, I pushed one finger inside her slick cunt.

She was laughing breathlessly, overwhelmed. "You're going so fast. Oh Jesus..."

I bit her neck. "Mmmm. Such pretty little panties. It's a shame they'll have to go."

I bunched my hand to rip them from her crotch. She grabbed my wrist. "Don't. Please don't. My sister gave them to me at my bachelorette party…"

I smiled inwardly, picturing Alexis giving Christina a set of snow-white lingerie. Probably with a joke about her wedding night.

Christina's words said one thing, but her hopeful eyes and sneaking smile said another. She'd worn the damn thong out of a sense of obligation.

"So you wore these panties to please her?" I smacked her ass again. "Well, she's not here. I am."

With one jerk, the fragile lace tore in my hand. Christina moaned in relief. I pushed the ruined panties down her thighs.

"Bend over, little lamb. Show me what I'm going to devour tonight."

Her hands shook as she braced them on the counter. Her dress frothed around her waist. I gave her luscious ass a slap.

"All the way."

Turning, she bent to touch the floor. Trembling with anticipation as she displayed her rosy cunt, glistening with arousal.

"Stay there," I ordered. "Hold onto your ankles."

She quivered, trying to keep still.

Dropping a hand on her thigh to anchor her, I cupped her pussy in my palm, using three fingers to caress her wet folds.

She whimpered, squirming under my attention. I could imagine how exposed she felt in this position, how vulnerable.

"Sshhh," I soothed. "You're a sweet little bride and I'm going to touch you here. I'm going to touch you everywhere before the night is over."

Christina was aroused and dripping, but wound up tight. As

she became accustomed to my touch, she spread her thighs, lifting her ass toward me. I smiled as her pussy opened like a velvety pink flower.

Increasing the pressure, I massaged her roughly, working her swollen clit between my fingers, savoring her moans and cries. Without warning, I sank two fingers into her tightness.

She moaned, bucking her hips, so eager that I curled my fingers to rub her G-spot. Her whole body was flushed. I was a big guy, huge hands, and I could imagine how full she felt.

"What's this?" My voice was soft and knowing. "The little bride isn't a virgin."

Her breath caught, and she shook her head. Her dark hair and gauzy veil hung around her face.

"You're not an innocent girl after all." I spread my fingers, stretching her hot pussy, twisting inside her as I pushed her toward the brink. "Did you fuck your husband early, sweetheart? Too impatient to wait for the wedding?"

"Goddammit, yes," she breathed, quivering under my possessive touch.

"Then it's a good thing I found you. Because I know exactly what to do with an impatient little girl."

"Please..." Her pussy tightened on my fingers, and she let out a long, helpless moan.

"Someone's turned on," I hissed. "It's been a long time, hasn't it, little lamb? Since you've been owned completely? Has your pussy forgotten what it feels like to be fingered? Don't worry, baby. I'll remind you."

Her juices spilled onto my hand as I plunged my fingers deeper into molten heat. I brought my thumb up to play with her clit, and she shuddered with pleasure.

She was approaching the edge. So I pulled my hand free. I

wanted to play with my prey first.

"What a good girl you are, showing me your pussy."

An inarticulate noise escaped her mouth. I took her supple ass cheeks in my hands and pried them apart, exposing her further.

"And what a naughty bride you are, offering your cunt to the wolf."

Fishing an ice cube from the bucket, I pressed the freezing chip against her tight opening. Christina groaned, her thighs flexing. Her veil floated above her back.

"No, no, don't move away, little lamb. I'm worried you'll overheat. Your pussy's so hot, this will all melt in no time. And you're going to hold still until it does."

She growled curses at me as I rubbed the cold cube over her lips and clit and pushed the last bit of the chip inside her. When I followed it with another, she shrieked. And another. Her pussy was beautiful: flushed, swollen, pulsing, every secret crevice displayed for me.

"I hate you," she gritted.

"Now, now," I crooned, "none of that."

I picked her up, swinging one arm under her knees and the other around her back, and tossed her on the bed. She landed with a thump, staring up at me,

"No, oh God no, not in the dress…"

We'd played with protesting before. I knew she'd use her safe word if she needed it. But to make sure, because that dress was fucking expensive, I grasped the voluminous skirt in my hands and looked into her pleading face.

"Hell yes, I'm going to take you in your wedding dress, girl. You're mine to do with as I please. Now turn over."

My gaze was cold, but I paused, giving her time to respond.

With some effort, she managed to roll into her stomach. The dress was tight, constricting her movements. Some nights, that would appeal. But tonight, I wanted her messy and thrashing and helplessly letting go.

I undid the bow at the back, pulled at the corset-style lacing, and slid the zipper open to her waist, admiring my handiwork. Much better. Without warning, I flipped up her foamy skirts again, baring her deliciously rounded ass.

A smack on one smooth cheek stained it with red. A sob left her mouth, and my vision blurred with arousal. My dick strained at my slacks.

"On my lap, princess."

She scrambled to obey, hampered by her half-undone gown. Dragging her over my lap, I pinned her glittering waist in place with my arm, the dark sleeve of my tux jacket contrasting with the trailing pale laces criss-crossing her warm brown skin.

Almost mindless with lust, I peppered her ass with smacks. She shrieked and writhed in my rough grasp.

"Why are you spanking me?" Tears glistened on her exquisitely made-up face. Her perfectly styled hair was turning into a tangled mess. "I've done everything you said."

"Oh, sweetheart." I massaged her glowing cheeks, pushing one hand between her thighs to rub her sensitive cunt. So hot, so slippery, excitement pulsing through her body. "I'm not punishing you. I'm just spanking you because I want to."

I gave her another hard smack, and she shuddered.

"I enjoy seeing you come apart on my lap. So helpless and aroused and so fucking honest. You can't be anything except the horny little girl you truly are." I spanked her luscious ass again, twice, soaking up her little gasps of protest. She squirmed against my dick, trapped in my tuxedo pants and hard as hell.

When her thighs parted, I slapped her pussy. She cried out.

"You want the wolf for your husband?"

"God, yes," she panted.

"Then there are going to be lots and lots and *lots* of spankings. Simply because I want to give them to you. I'm going to take you and keep you and use you as I wish."

I rained more smacks on her ass, emphasizing each word, while she bit the bedspread to muffle her yelps.

Taking pity, I flipped her onto her back on the hotel bed, pushing her snowy skirts out of the way to expose her slick pussy. I wasted no time sinking two fingers inside her, teasing her cruelly by barely flicking her clit.

"It's so much," she moaned. Her skin glistened with a faint sheen of sweat.

"And you're close to coming, aren't you?" I pressed harder on her slippery clit. "I know how you take your pleasure. Little slut."

She gripped my wrist as I eased my fingers out of her tightness. "Don't stop…"

"But we have to celebrate, sweet one. I couldn't let this night pass without all the romance you want."

She sat upright as I threw off my jacket and rolled up my sleeves. I loved the pinkness rising on her skin. When I really got to Christina, got under her skin, she glowed. With a mix of nerves, arousal, vulnerability, love.

I brought the bottle of champagne and the bouquet of roses to the bed.

"You're so eager to come? Touch yourself. With this."

I tossed a red rose between her spread legs. Trembling, she took it and rubbed the soft petals over her soaked cunt, knowing it would only make the teasing worse.

Popping the cork on the champagne, I shook my head.

"You didn't even open this. I'll have to enjoy it with my main course." I pulled down her stiff corset-shaped top. Her bare breasts sprang free, ready to be marked.

"Please..." Her eyes were wide with excitement, but she clutched the foamy dress to her body. "You'll make a mess."

"I absolutely will." I knew how she responded to my cruel tone of voice. Desperately aroused, wet and dripping. "And so will you. You're a mess, Christina. You always have been."

She moaned, her full lips parting, and caught her bottom lip between her teeth.

Some girls would be insulted, furious at my choice of words. They'd want kisses and compliments. But when I called Christina a mess, it helped her let go of the mantle of perfectionism she'd fought all her life. It didn't show up as much now, but it lurked.

"Keep touching your pussy with that pretty flower, baby. It tickles, doesn't it? I know it's driving you insane. It's not even close to what you truly need."

Cupping her tit in my hand, pinching the dark point of her nipple, I spilled bubbly over her skin. She hissed at the snap of the fizz, grabbed my hair, and let out a cry as it soaked her dress.

"Fuck."

"It's a relief, isn't it, sweet bride? To finally let go?"

Unthinking, I bent my head to suck her nipples. When I captured one puckered bud, the yeasty taste of champagne filled my mouth.

My mind swirled. This was my first taste of alcohol in almost three years. I hadn't been thinking straight, I'd been thinking about Christina and how to drive her wild, and now I was sucking champagne off my wife's tits and the flavor was hitting my brain and desire roared through my body for all my drugs of choice.

"Patrick?" She grabbed my head and looked into my eyes. Her arousal was pushed aside by concern. "Patrick, you don't have to do this."

"I want to."

"Listen to me." Her tone grew more urgent. "I love you." She cupped my jaw. "I love you so, so much. I can't even put it into words. Whatever you do, it's going to feel good. Don't tempt yourself just to make me happy."

I looked at her sprawled beneath me. Her rumpled wedding gown, pushed down around her waist and up around her hips. Dark hair lacquered into her wedding style, but loosened, pearl hairpins falling out and scattered over the pillow. A red rose lying between her legs, petals tipped with her juices.

The love of my life.

Slowly, deliberately, I bent my head.

"You're my temptation, Christina," I whispered. "My guilty pleasure. Nothing else will ever match that. All I want is you."

I sucked on her hard nipple. When I used my teeth, she moaned. She was so sweet, so tender. So hot and alive. My awareness of the alcohol receded to the background, evaporating into the air.

Blindly, I found the discarded rose and dragged the petals over her thigh. She squirmed beneath me.

"You're all I want, Patrick," she murmured.

"That's my girl."

I kissed her between the breasts and unknotted my bowtie. She stared hungrily as I stripped off my shirt and tossed it aside.

"Turn over."

She rolled over wantonly, lifting her ass in the air, spreading her cheeks to give me an unfettered view of her pussy while she peeked over her shoulder with a naughty grin.

Love surged through me. It made me so happy to see her like this. Delighted, unashamed and open.

But I gave her a swift slap on the ass, because I knew that would make her even happier. And another on the other cheek, so they'd both glow.

"Please…fuck me." Her husky voice quavered with need.

"I will, baby." I got off the bed and stood. "Close your eyes. Be a good girl and don't peek."

She squeezed her eyes shut, her lips curving in a smile of anticipation.

Kissing the top of her head, I took in the image of my beautiful bride. Her perfect makeup was smudged. Black mascara streaked under her eyes, pink lipstick sucked off, the sheen of sex and sweat glistening on her skin. Her veil floated over her bare back with its half-unlaced ribbons. Her champagne-soaked dress, the top pushed down and the skirts flipped up, frothed around her waist and hips.

She tensed, on her hands and knees, her bare ass in the air.

Waiting for me.

My belt and slacks hit the floor. I pulled off my boxers. I ached, fucking ached, to bury myself inside her. I wanted her more than I'd ever wanted anyone or anything.

I found what I needed in my duffel bag. Kneeling between her spread legs, I squeezed her supple ass in one hand and squirted the lube onto her tight pucker.

"Shit," she gasped, jerking in surprise.

"Mmm. There's something so dirty about this. Isn't there?" I traced my finger deliberately down her cleft. Slowly, gently, I caressed her asshole. "Your ass spread for me, your pretty, snowy, pure white wedding dress flipped up, while you wait for me to take my pleasure."

"God, Patrick…" she panted.

"I'm going to fuck your ass tonight, little lamb. I want you exactly like this."

"Please," she pleaded, sliding a shameless finger into her cunt.

I laughed. "Poor baby. Just look at you. Your pussy's hungry too…all pink and swollen and dripping with girl cum. Hmm. Which hole should I fuck first?"

Christina looked over her shoulder, her eyes deep and dark enough to drown in. "Whatever you want, take it, Patrick. It's yours."

I gripped her ass. "Damn right."

She squeezed her eyes shut, waiting, and let out a moan when I sank into her inviting pussy. She was so wet, so hot and excited, she took me easily from behind in a single thrust.

"Yes…so good…"

"You want me to fuck you like I did our first time? Now that you're my wife?"

She cried out, and her hips bucked eagerly. Our first time had been intense, aggressive, even angry on Christina's part. Complicated, with so much wanting underneath.

I pushed her face into the bed, reveling in the rush of power. I held still so I wouldn't come too soon.

Suddenly, she jerked against my grasp, trying to free herself. It felt genuine, not playful.

"Evergreen," she gritted into the pillow. Our safe word.

Startled, I let her go.

"It's not like the first time." She twisted her head to look up at me. "It's absolutely nothing like the first time. Because I love you now."

I froze. Couldn't speak. Because the force of my feelings for her hit me like a tidal wave.

My hand cradled her cheek. "I love you too, Christina."

"Please fuck the hell out of me."

I did.

As she moaned and writhed, shoving back at me, gripping the pillow with pearly nails, I didn't know if we were descending into the earth like rutting animals, or soaring above it to exalt this night.

It took all my strength to leave her cunt. To pull out, coat my cock in lube, and rub the head against her sweet ass. To keep it slow as I opened her yielding flesh. She lifted her hips, adjusting to my size.

"Come on, baby," she whispered. So much more open, more upfront, than when we met. "I need all of you."

"Fuck, you're a greedy whore. You can't get enough."

She inhaled sharply, and her ass clutched my cock. I'd used a filthy mouth with her from the beginning, and she'd lapped it up. But I hadn't called her that name in months. Our fucking had become all softness, all sweetness.

But Christina needed both. She needed the teddy bear and the wolf.

And I needed to be them with her.

"Aren't you, Christina? Say it," I said harshly.

When I pressed her clit, rubbing insistently, she shivered and whimpered.

"God, yes. Yes, I am. I'm yours, Patrick, I'll do whatever you want…"

I kissed her shoulder, running my hungry mouth over smooth skin, as I eased my cock deeper into her velvety tightness. "My wife. *Mine.*"

She let out a soundless cry, squeezing me in a long spasm, losing herself in the sensations as she finally came.

I stopped holding back. Gripping her hips, I fucked my love, giving her everything I had.

Everywhere.

Always.

She arched her back as I came in her ass. My lamb, my angel, my slut, my bride.

Afterward, she stripped away the rest of the layers. The makeup, the hairpins. I helped her out of the dress. We showered together, exhausted and sated.

"Hey, husband," she whispered once we were in bed together. "You're back. Where'd the wolf go?"

I traced the shape of her heart on her flesh. "Right here."

A smile lit up her clean-scrubbed face. "God, you're mushy." She twined her arms around me and leaned her head against my chest.

I rubbed her shoulders. Worn out as we were, I couldn't resist teasing her.

"You know you didn't have to wear those fancy panties, right, baby? Your sister would have understood."

Her eyes narrowed. "Why do you think I did? I was hoping you'd rip them. Now I have a beautiful souvenir."

I laughed and caressed her wet hair. "Good start? You think we're going to have a good life together?"

"I couldn't ask for better."

"I love you so much, Christina," I whispered, as she drifted off.

"Love you too, my wolf," she mumbled into my chest. "Forever."

ACKNOWLEDGEMENTS

Big thanks to Jan Saenz, my brilliant and delightful critique partner, for her ongoing feedback and love.

To Michelle Clay, for being a fairy godmother.

To Book Nerd Services, run by Michelle and the amazing Annette Brignac, for their professionalism, creativity, and unflagging support.

To Betty Lankovits, for bringing her artistic vision to the cover and graphics.

To Crystal Leann Glover, for suggesting the premise of "Teach Me."

To all the early readers of *Crave*, for their enthusiasm and encouragement.

And always, to my husband.

ABOUT THE AUTHOR

Miranda Silver writes sexy stories with a twist. She's happy to be putting her English degree to use, along with her love of drama, secrets, steam, and words. Miranda lives on the West Coast with her family, where she spends time outdoors whenever possible. Her other books include *The Boys Next Door, The Girl in Between,* and *Priceless.*

mirandasilver.com
Facebook.com/MirandaSilverBooks
Instagram: @mirandasilverbooks
Twitter: @silvermusings

Made in the USA
Coppell, TX
09 May 2023

16633606R00094